Slime Season

By: Kevin "OLA KEN" Durham

ACKNOWLEDGEMENT

First off, all praises to Allah, the Most High period to my parents Leonard (Skinner) and Linda, my king and queen. I honor you and praise you. Without your love for each other I wouldn't be here, and none of this would be possible. You are no longer with us physically, but I feel you both in my spirit, guiding me, and pulling me up when I stumble.

To my beautiful queen Sonya, you brought so much greatness to my life. You kept me focus and grounded. I feel your love flowing through my veins and empowering my very being. You my Snooky doodle, 4 life.

To my one and only daughter, Wilena Hollis (NeeNee). you the beat of my heart the first human to motivate me to be the best version of myself. Throughout the years, I was gone a lot, and I want to apologize for that, but you was the first and last thought in my head I had every single day. You have grown to be an amazing woman, wife, and mother. Thank you, for giving me three of the coolest grandsons in the world, DJ, King, and Aiden. And for the prettiest granddaughter, baby Ivy. Also, I want to say thank you to my son in law, Dante Hollis. You are a real gentleman, you did it right, and I couldn't have picked a better mate for my daughter than you.

To my son, my namesake, my twin, Kevin Durham Jr (KJ). you are the son I prayed for it, and I vow by Allah, I will always have your back. When I look in your eyes, I now Feel what my dad Felt when he saw me. You are a cool kid ow, but you will grow up to be a great man, one day. You're the gift for all the right I've done. I love you, son.

To my aunt Mary and uncle David (R.I.P). there are not enough words to say what needs to be said. I won't ever forget what y'all did. I love y'all period to my aunt Melva, I call my

Momtie. Thanks for holding the family down. You have always treated me like your very own child, and I'm so grateful for you. I love you, Momtie. To my brother, Head. You my twin brother from another mother. Your mom, Ms. Betty, Have always treated me like a second son, and I love her for that. Your sisters, Tocka, Keyanna, and Pam, are my sisters too. Aye my nigga, Thanks for holding me down and being a real one. You the bro I never doubted, and I love you for that my nigga.

To my bro Flame, thanks for being a real soldier, and keeping it slime, you feel me? I be who you be, you be who I be. Before they kill you, they gotta kill me. Slatt!

To my baby brother Ricky (R.I.P) I miss you my nigga. every move I make, I do it in your honor. You gone, but never forgotten. How can I forget you, when I got your name tatted on my face.

My two sisters Anisha and Minnie. Y'all my babies yo, and I love you both equally. I'm thankful for you all being here when I need y'all. A lot of people don't answer the phone when the calls come, but y'all do. Thanks to my big bro, Pistol Pete, you the one and only, King Slime! East side to the royal flesh. To my big homie Nasty (Slime Lord), drip or drown, all green everything. Free the real: OLA Nasty, OLA Nut, OLA Mac-II, OLA E.T. Hock, OLA Tyson. I was blessed to be in your presence and view the flame through your eyes. SLATT!

Last but not least, to the realest hood I know, Summerhill, also known as the red zone. This where you go to get stamped, you already know. We official tissue over this way. ⸙

I couldn't go without saying a few names: Felipe, Bemo, Big Gerald, Killa Corey (KC), Smitty, Dana Lundy, VeeVee, Fonda, Tiffany, New Edition, Taylor Dane, Kato, Inda, Popcorn, Bayboy, Big Bam, Almeata, Sabrina, FatBoy, Black James, Randy Brooks, Bloody Jay, Gucci, K.T, Squat, Lac, Major Gram, The Diablos (Lil Relb, Scott, and Chop) O.B, Montae, Squirt. Keith, Lucci, Shell, Bapo, Norris, Straw, Fat and Kay. My bro Doe, EL, Ruckus, J Cartier, Extra, Doe Shay, AJ (Mr.1000) Lil Dennis, Head, Richie rich, and the whole Click Treal.

Dedications:

To the ones that couldn't finish the journey with me. Mom, dad, Grandma Essie, Mary, David, Mouth, Ricky, KayKay, Robert, Rose, Grover, Henry, Quint, Jeremiah, Duke, Pretty tony, Nut, Small, Walt Forte, Rob Base, Dino, Freda, Lashonda, A-Baby, Lil Tim, Shaheed, Kentray, Kuatavious, Kevondre, Kua'necia, Lil Kevin, Man, Thad, Paul, Michael Dozier, Tracy (Tre-8), Ms. Rose, Norris Duffy, Monkey Man, Lil Tab, Ms. Betty, Corey Brown (pop), Aunt Barbera, Ms. Dot, Big Wayne, (Dank), Kelcie, Wezone and, Klack… Gone but not forgotten.

CHAPTER 1

Khalif Flournoy, better known as Supa to all that know him, looked around the prison parking lot after just being released from Telfair state prison- a high max prison located in South Georgia.

His eyes scanned over the parking lot looking for his girlfriend, Danielle who was supposed to be out front waiting on him. She was a Georgia transplant, originally from New York City.

One of his blood homies from Brooklyn that was also locked up at Telfair, had introduced Supa to Danielle, by the end of Supa's sentence, he and Danielle had become very close. She proved to be very loyal to Supa, something he haven't seen in the woman he knew in his past.

Danielle, was very beautiful Italian, from a wealthy family. And she spoiled supa and provided him with anything he asked for.

Three months prior to his release, Danielle, also called Danny by her family, relocated to Atlanta to be with Supa.

She purchased a luxury condominium for them

in the north Atlanta upscale community, Alpharetta.

She got the new Dodge Challenger Hellcat that he asked for, Plus a brand-new wardrobe.

Finally, his eyes locked on Danielle running towards him. She hopped into his arms and gave him a big wet kiss.

"Whoa baby!"

I was able to say between kisses.

"You a big girl," I say jokingly, as I balance all of Danielle's 5"11, 160-pound frame in my arms.

"Boy whatever," she says in her New York accent.

Danielle was a true amazon- tall, with ass and hips like a black girl. She has long brown hair, hazel eyes, and juicy lips- like Angelina Jolie.

And she was lookin' really sexy in white-leggings and a tank-top that barely covered her ample breast.

After reluctantly breaking off our kiss, we strolled hand in hand to the white Hellcat challenger.

"Damn, this bitch clean!" I say excitedly lookin' at the car over.

"I told you I had you bae," she said.

"I can't wait to get my license reinstated so I can push it!" I say gettin' in on the passenger-side.

'I got something for you to push, and you don't need a license to do it," she responded with a sexy smile.

I laugh, "Shid baby, you aint said nothin'. Especially seein' what I saw on my phone."

Danielle sent me a sexy video to my phone of her playin' in her pussy with a dildo.

Once we hit the highway, she opened up the motor and did the dash to get us home.

The next morning, I woke up with a big smile on my Face, happy I was home in my own bed and not a cell.

I looked over at Danielle, still asleep next to me. My smile grew even bigger, remembering all the freaky things we did last night.

When we first entered the condo, we tore off each other's clothes.

now just lookin' at her layin' on top of the cover, with her perfectly tanned body exposed to my eyes, I feel myself getting' hard.

I reach over and slide two fingers in between her shaved pussy lips. I suck one nipple into my mouth and bite down lightly.

"Sss. Mmm," she moan's as her eyes open.

No more words were spoken as I eased my body on top of her, and then push my pole deep into her moist pussy. I place her legs over my shoulders as I grind and pump. I feel her walls contracting around my meat, makin' me drill harder and faster.

Moments later, I cum deep inside her pussy.

Later on, that same day, after leaving the DMV with my license, I dropped Danielle back off at home.

I drive over to Summer hill, to link up with the homies to let everyone know I was out.

As I ride down Hank Aaron Drive, I notice all the changes that was made to my hood.

Old houses that was once familiar to me had been knocked down or replaced by newer Town homes and stores.

Turnin' on Haygood Avenue, I immediately see the Bloods posted up in Boynton Village Apartments.

Everybody was wearin' somethin' red along with a red flag hangin' from their right back pocket.

As they spot me pullin' into the parkin' lot they all started throwin' up the B with their fingers, as a respect For the Bloods.

"Whooh!" I say as I hop out the challenger.

All the homies said it back to me as we peace up and show love.

"Damn, big homie we happy you back!" says a tall dark-skinned dude with a red bandana tied around his dreads.

"Hell yeah, it's been too long, Blood," I say to

the dude speakin', known as Bloody Tye.

"since you was gone, we held the set down and kept the hood popin', ya smell me?" Bloody Tye said to me.

I nod my head, "Yeah I smell you Blood."

Everybody was ice'd out and fresh in designer clothes, From head to toe. Also, I noticed all the cars sittin' on 24's or better in the parking lot and it hit me that I had to step my game up.

While I was in prison, some of the homies had started doin' music, and from what I could see, it was payin' off.

As we stood around catchin' up, a black 7 series BMW pulled in. A man jumped out wearin' more diamonds than most rappers.

"What's poppin' Blood?" the man asks.

"Us fuck them!" states one of the homies.

The man proceeds to walk toward me, and as he got closer a smile spread across his face.

"Wassup big homie, how B?" says the man to me.

Smiling' back, "shid bruh, I'm boolin' happy to be out," I respond, and we peace'd up and embraced.

"Aye shell, I really appreciate you makin' sure my sis and nephew was straight," I tell the homie, Shell.

Shell, nods his head, "Ain't no thang, Blood," he reply.

"Oh, and before I forget, I got somethin' in the car for you, too."

Shell, walks to the BMW and then returned with a gold Gucci link, with the A.B.G medallion on it. My face lights up as I see the iced-out pendant.

"Good lookin', for holdin' it down for me, Blood!" I said as he returned my chain to me. I put it around my neck, and it feels like I'm really back now.

Now, let's get this money, I think to myself...

CHAPTER 2

After bein' home in prison for a few months, I'm back in full grind mode. Before my release, Danielle, managed to save up to $26,000 dollars for me.

The money came from managing one of her uncle's bars in Manhattan.

I also had been sellin' weed while I was in prison, was able to put away $10,000 dollars. So, when I came home, I didn't have to ask a nigga for anything.

I least the building in the hood that was once a grocery- store. I reopened it and renamed it the Red-Zone variety store.

Whether you want a groceries or work- it was always available.

While I was standin' outside the store talkin' to a couple lil' homies, a Gray 2015 Camaro pull up and park in the back of the store, and the driver gets out and walks towards me.

"What's blazing bruh?" he asked me as we lock guns in the sex money murda handshake.

"We blazing," I state. "What you got going' on, Smoke?"

"Check this out bruh," Smoke says as we step to the side away from the other homies. "I was just out there on Bouldercrest, fuckin round wit' the homie Chrome," he starts to explain. "And that nigga lil' Ced, pull up on us shootin' craps. A few of them brick squad niggas was out there gambling' wit' us too, and lil' Ced, starting kickin' that sucka shit, talkin' bout why y'all lettin' these Summerhill niggas be over here gettin' money, this ain't Haygood, this the 'Crest"

Upon hearin' this my face screwed up in a scowl. Smoke, continues, "he was tripping' bruh, I wasn't feeling that shit at all, Chrome, had to slick stop me from puttin' that fie' on that nigga!"

I chuckled at that statement because I knew how hotheaded smoke can get.

Something had to be done about lil' Ced, and that sneak-dissin' shit. But it had to be done in a way, so it didn't look like we had beef with the bricksquad.

In truth, we fucks wit' each other the long way-their boss got the A.B.G tatted under his eye.

"But anyway bruh, this what I came to tell you," Smoke, said gettin' to the point. "While we was gamblin', that nigga looked like he had bricks stuffed in all four pockets, no cap!"

My eyes light up at hearing that revelation, and my mind went straight to robbin' mode. I was stackin' gwapo off the lil' work I sold- but I wouldn't pass up the chance for some easy paper- especially from a big mouth fuck nigga!

Smoke goes on to say, "Chrome, be out there on the 'crest wit them niggas, and he say ole boy be havin' Them racks on him every day, always tryin' to flex on niggas."

I nod my head at what Smoke was tellin' me.

"Yeah, I already know how he do," I interjected.

"Me and Five was at the Flame last week, and he came through wit' three other niggas, buyin' the bar and throwin' money, on some fake ass BMF shit."

Laughin', Smoke said, "that's what I'm sayin' bruh, we might as well spank that baby, show 'em what A.B.G stands for."

After we spoke for a few moments longer, Smoke, leaves to catch a play.

I go back into the store and ponder on the best way to catch lil' Ced slippin' so I can rob him.

As I was deep in thought, my phone rings, and I see Danielle's face pop up on the screen.

"Hey baby, what's good?" I answer my phone.

"Nothin' much," she says, via skype. "I was just checkin' on you, since it seems you too busy to check on me," she states playfully.

As usual, her makeup was on fleek, hair was flawless, lookin' beautiful.

"I aint on nothin', just doin' what I do, ya feel me? but, I'm never too busy for yo' sexy ass!"

Her face beams at the compliment, "you better not be if you know what's good for you," she jokingly says. "when are you comin' home, bae? I miss you."

"Umm... I should be done in a couple of hours Okay."

"Okay baby," she said happily. "See you soon," she made the kiss face, then ended the Skype-call.

A few days after speakin' with smoke about Lil' Ced, I got in contact with Chrome, and had him pull up at Red Zone.

We discussed the best time and place to rob lil' Ced.

Lil' Ced, had a trap house on a side-street, off Bouldercrest road, and thru-out the day, him and one of his workers but walk up to the Texaco, gas-station to buy blunts.

Texaco, it's a major meetin' place for all the dope boys on Bouldercrest road, and the traffic be thick in the parkin' lot, and most of the niggas they're got guns placed all around the store, for easy access.

With that bein' the case, it would be suicide to try and rob lil' Ced at the Texaco.

But once he leaves and walks back to his trap house, he's a sittin' duck-him and his worker.

Once I got all the info on lil' Ced, I put a team together. We were parked in Eagles landing apartment complex, on Bouldercrest Road. We was waitin' on a phone-call from Chrome, to let us know when lil' Ced start walkin' towards his trap house.

"You know what to do right?" I asked from the passenger-seat of the black Tahoe.

The driver nods, "Yeah."

The third passenger sits quietly in the back seat. He had a stony expression on his face as he checks to make sure his gun was off- safety, and ready.

My phone rings, it's Chrome, he had been posted at Texaco, waitin' to spot lil' Ced

"That duck in motion," Chrome confirms. "They just crossed the street, walkin."

"Aight bruh," I reply then hang up.

I look at the driver," let's go, we got action."

As we drove up Bouldercrest Road, I speak to the homie in the backseat.

"Aye Ra Ra, make sure you grab the nigga walkin' wit lil' Ced"

We drive pass Texaco and bear right on Fayetteville Road, and that's where we spot the two men walkin'.

I notice lil' Ced has his phone to his ear, not payin' attention to his surroundings.

We pull right next to them, and out jumps me and RaRa. I point my AK-47 at lil' Ced, and he take off runnin', but I took off right behind him, and after a short run, he turns around quickly, grabbin' for the barrel of the AK-47, tryin' to snatch it from my hands.

"Boom. Boom." Two bullets tear into the flesh off lil' Ced's right thigh and hip. he let out a scream and falls to the ground.

I point the assault-rifle at his head.

"Please don't kill me!" lil' Ced begs. "here, take it!" lil' Ced, painfully takes his pants off that was stuffed with money.

The choppa' destroyed the Robin jeans lil' Ced was wearin', exposin' the ripped-up flesh and bone.

Once I got the bloody pants, I turn and run back to the awaitin' Tahoe.

I see RaRa, standin' over the other nigga, with his F and N pointed at the back of his head.

We get in the truck after RaRa left the man face-down, with his shirt pulled over his head. Driving off, I still heard lil' Ced cryin' in the street, beggin' someone to help him.

ATL summers, are always super-lit! The day-parties, are poppin' off at different clubs and bars, mad people out havin' fun!

Every year around summer, each neighborhood thru-out the city has their hood-day.

Hood-day, be the most talked about and anticipated event of the summer- it ranks high, up there with the birthday bash, and street Fest!

Different types of events go on at hood-day- from rap-battles, twerk-contest, dance-battles to all the kid friendly-games. The older residents of the neighborhood had the grills burnin' makin' sure everyone had good food to eat.

The hood-day rarely turns violent because the different clicks that come thru from other 'hoods, or in some way connected to each other- either thru Street-ties, gang-ties or music-ties-so for the most part, it's all love.

This Saturday, it is Summerhill-day, and the streets are out. Everyone is kickin' it at the park on Georgia Avenue.

Children, runnin' all over the park. Too many bad bitches to count wearin' the sexiest, skimpiest outfits they could find. some of the outfits I saw on these ho's revealed more naked skin then strippers at Magic City.

I was sitting in a lawn-chair inside the Super-large red tent, that's the homies set up every year.

On the basketball court, there is a giant banner tied from one goal across the court to the other goal. the banner is white with the A.B.G logo in red on it.

Even though there are a few different squads that come from Summerhill – the whole city knows that Summerhill belongs to A.B.G.

"It's hot as shit!" I exclaim.

"Hell yeah," Bloody Tye, agrees. "This bitch on fie', today."

"This shit packed like the Georgia Dome, it looked like everybody in the city came thru!" said Shell, entering the tent.

I stand up to stretch my legs and to take a look outside the tent.

I see my ex, Goldie, approaching me, walkin' with another girl- a super-bad red-bone!

Goldie was my first love, from childhood. I had taken her virginity when she was 12 and I was 13.

Goldie, No longer dealt with men, she turned lesbian and a few years ago- but she still had a soft spot for me.

"Wassup, fly-guy?" Goldie greets me with a hug. "I see you still givin' these ho's somethin' to look at." commenting on my Dior outfit.

"Shid baby you know how I do it," I pop back.

I had hit the Lenox mall earlier that mornin', and copped the beige and white Christian Dior loafers, beige A'merie jeans and a white Dior T shirt. I capped my ft off wit' the elephant Tusk Cartier frames.

I also got my dreads dyed blonde and put up in a Man-bun, hairstyle.

I was lookin' like a boss playa and the ho's was sweatin' me hard as they passed by.

"Aye but check game tho. I see you still puttin' that shit together like I taught you," I said jokingly, admiring Goldie's Fendi short set, with matchin' Fendi tennis shoes.

"Boy whatever!" she retorted with a smile,

showing' her gold and diamond grill. "Give me my props, you know I inspire you when it comes to this designer shit."

"Pop yo' shit then, lil' buddy," I reply with a laugh. "We're gone change yo' name from Goldie, to lil' Supa."

"Anyway, what you got planned for later?" she asked me.

"Everybody, supposed to be hittin' Brucial after the reunion," I say, referrin' to club crucial, one of the hottest night clubs on the West side of Atlanta-located on Bankhead Hwy. "why, wassup?"

Goldie looks at me with a mischievous grin.

"Because I want you to come thru and kick it with me tonight. You aint rocked with me since you been home, and I feel away," she says. "Plus, I've got a surprise for you, too!"

I agree to fall thru after I leave the club.

Everybody, begin walkin' towards the tennis court, where the stage was set up for YFN Lucci, to perform.

Later that night...

Before I pulled out the club parkin' lot, I texted Goldie, to let her know I was on my way.

Danielle, was still in New York, handlin' some family business, and wouldn't be back for a few days.

I didn't want to be home alone, so Goldie's invitation for me to come thru was on time.

At this late hour, Bankhead Hwy. Was mostly void of traffic. It felt like I was glidin' on air, in the red Hellcat, floatin' on 26-inch davins -catchin' all the green lights as I shot up Bankhead Hwy.

The new paint- job, plus the rims and music, was all paid for from the $60,000 me and RaRa took from Lil' Ced and his worker, over a month ago. The split was 20 racks apiece.

Goldie has a condo downtown Marietta Blvd, so I stopped at a Chevron gas station, down the street from her apartment, and bought a backwood and a five-hour energy.

After parkin' in the garage, I take the elevator to her floor.

Goldie opens the door in a pair of heels and a red thong.

I admire all the tattoos she has gotten'. She don't have as many as me, but still a lot.

"Hey baby! Goldie said. "I'm glad you came and didn't stand me up.

She pulls me over to the sectional and sits next to me.

"Nah, I wouldn't play you like that," I reply. "I Fuck wit' you."

Goldie smiles upon hearin' that.

"Do you got a light, so I can Fie' this blunt up?" I ask, as I roll up.

"Yeah, hold up" she walks to her bedroom.

I notice the sounds of H.E.R. comin' from the bedroom.

"Here you go," she hands me a lighter.

She sits back down and places her legs over my lap, and I rub her thighs as I Smoke.

When I finished smokin' my gas-blunt, I downed the 5-hour energy drink.

She laughs and say, "I see you came prepared for a long night.

"Hell yeah, I Know you an animal! I was wit' you for years before we broke up."

"Facts!" Goldie agrees, as she rubs my dick thru my jeans. "Then you already know how I get down, Mr. Supa."

She grabs my hand, "come on baby" And pulls me towards her bedroom.

I was hypnotized at how her ass bounced and jiggled as she walked in Front of me.

"Surprise bae!" Goldie, says excitedly." Here's your late, welcome home present. I hope you like it"

My eyes light up, as I stare lustfully at the sexy ass redbone, layin' on the bed naked, rubbin' on her pussy lips.

"Damn!" I state with a big smile.

I recognized the sexy red bone, from earlier with Goldie, at the reunion in Summer hill.

Goldie, sits down on the bed and then scoots back until she was next to the red bone.

Goldie slowly slid her thong down her legs.

I stood at the foot of the bed, watchin' her and the red bone rub each other's pussy.

They were lickin' the juice from each other's fingers and moanin' like it was the best thing they ever tasted.

Goldie, eyes my dick print with lust.

"Damn, Diamond it looks like Supa ready to play with us," Goldie, states with a gleam.

Diamond, crawls on all fours to the edge of the bed. She unbuckle my Dior belt, and pulls my hard pole out, and start suckin, deep-throatin' it like a porn-star. She was spittin' on it and slurpin' it back up.

Goldie, was watchin us and rubbin' her large, swollen clit.

I quickly take off my clothes and lay back on the Versace Covers.

Goldie climbs on top of my dick, as Diamond bends over and sat her bald pussy in my face.

"Shit!" Goldie groans as she ride's my dick.

"MMMM," she moans. "Damn, you feel good!"

Diamonds, pussy is so wet, it's leavin' a wet trail runnin' down my face, stainin the covers.

"Suck this pussy, daddy!" Diamond, tells me as she grind on my lips. "I want to cum on your tongue."

Diamond starts moanin' louder, "Yes! Yes! ...I'm Cummin!" She says as she releases a stream of cum in my mouth.

"Make this pussy cum," Goldie chant's over

and over, before she explodes, "Ah shit...here it comes baby!"

Before Goldie could catch her breath from bustin' a big nut, I bend her over, ass up, face, down, I hit her soakin' pussy mercilessly.

"Yes daddy, fuck this pussy!" she begs, throwin it back. "Oooh, that dick feels good!"

"You miss this shit don't you?" I say as I smack her across her ass.

"Mmhm," she moans while bitin her lower lip.

"Shit!" I exclaim, as I pull out and bust a load of cum on Goldie's ass cheeks.

CHAPTER 3

Today, was like any other day in the hood; Junkies all around, movin' fast, tryin' to come up on a few dollars, to get a blast.

Ho's walkin' up and down the block, sweatin' niggas in the trap. Most of the neighborhood scram, we done already fucked on-so we good on them now— we be tryin' to hit that new shit when it come our way.

Aint nothin' better than fuckin' bitches from other 'hoods. Some niggas be thinkin they have papers on the neighborhood thots and be hatin' when niggas from other hoods come thru and fuck them ho's. I'm glad I'm a playa and not a sucka, so I just be laughin' at lames.

The block is hot, wit' niggas shootin craps on the apartment steps. Ho's hangin around, tryin to see who winnin', so they can try to trick a young nigga out some money.

The police creepin thru, tryin to scare niggas off, but that shit ain't bout nothin-niggas still workin' non-stop.

I was Taught that if your block ain't hot, then you must not be gettin' money. So, I say fuck Twelve, let 'em do their jobs, and I'm goin to do mines.

They ain't nothin' but crabs, hatin' on niggas shine. Mad cause we ridin around in these foreign cars, drippin in Ice.

It's So bad here in the A, that the Feds have set up surveillance, outside Neiman Marcus, Motor-Sports car expo, and Ice-box Jeweler, in Buckhead- Takin' pictures of niggas comin' and goin'.

They hate all the illegal money bein' spent on cars, jewelry, and clothes.

I got my car parked in Boynton Village, and I'm leanin' up against the hood.

I'm drippin in designer everything: Black Balmain Joggers, black and red Balenciaga's Tennis shoes, with a fitted black V-neck T-shirt, by Michael Kors.

I look up from my phone, to see a white Audi truck pull in next to my challenger.

"Hey Supa! Wassup Sexy?" A girl said from the window of the Audi,

"Shid, ayn on nothin," I reply to the girl as she gets out the truck and give me a hug.

"What you Doin over this way, Dominique?"

"I just came from my friend house, she stays around the corner, on Hill Street," she explains.

"I saw your car as I drove by and pulled up to say hi."

Dominique always had a crush on me from before I got locked up. I used to trap out a Duplex across from her house.

Every time I use to pull up, she would come out on her porch and speak to me.

She was a super thick red bone, with dimples that resembled Laura London, when she smiled.

She was wearin' a cat-suit that hugged her frame like a second skin.

I can tell she Didn't have any underwear on, not even a bra. The material of the cat-suit was cuttin' up between her pussy-lips, makin a camel-toe.

She saw how my eyes kept lookin' down at her pussy print, while we were talkin'.

"What's wrong?" she asked with a sexy smile, and a knowin' look.

I shake my head.

"Ain't nothin wrong," I say, "I'm just tryin' to figure out how that nigga let you out the house like that."

She laughed; knowin' I was referring to her fat pussy print.

"First off, I ain't got no nigga. And secondly, it don't matter what I wear, my pussy fat regardless." She glanced down at my joggers, before continuing, "I can say the same thing to you, I can see your dick print thru your joggers."

I laugh at her slick mouth, and quick comeback.

She then says, "If you got a problem with my pussy bein so fat, then do somethin' about it."

"Shawdy, you hell!" I say. "You gone make me fuck the air out yo' ass."

"Yeah, whatever," she responds.

"Nah for real," I come back.

"Mmhm, I hear you talkin' lil buddy," she said, rollin' her eyes at me, playfully.

She asked for my phone to program her number in it.

"Well, you got my number, so don't be a stranger," she said handin' my phone back.

I nod my head.

"I'm stoppin' by my mom's for a minute, but hit me later, okay," she tells me, as she gets in her truck and leaves.

Two of my long time partnas hit me up about a lick they had been layin' on, and they wanted me in on it with them.

We were now on our way to Stone Mountain, a Suburb area, in East Atlanta.

Me, Dae, and Jay D, have done plenty licks together in the past, and we been close Friend's since the sandbox. I trusted them with my life, and it was vice-versa, For them.

I really didn't have to go on this mission, because I wasn't really pressed for cash at the moment. I actually had a lil' over a hundred racks put up, from trappin' and a few joogs I been catchin' - plus my store was makin' a few bands, a week.

But I Know everybody aint in the same financial position—and things could change for the worst, very quickly. One minute you up, and the next you down.

So, when my partnas' hit me up— I agreed to assist them on this caper, because I never know when I might need them, to help me buss a move- and from what they told me- the money was too good to pass up.

We was on our way to rob a Jamaican named Sun Sun, which was movin' a lot of weed on the East Side. After doin' our homework on him, we found out he had weed spots in Decatur, Lithonia, Scottdale and Stone Mountain.

A lot of robbers that came from the zones of Atlanta, rarely traveled that deep into Dekalb County. So, the hustlers from the suburbs of Metro-Atlanta, are more hidden, than hustlers that moved work thru the inner-city of Atlanta.

But bein' a jack-boy, puts you in rotation with Niggas all over the city, and that's how the Jamaican, Sun Sun, came across our path.

Another partna of ours that use to be in the streets doin' dirt wit' us, had moved with his wife and Kids to Stone Mountain— and just so happen the house he bought is across the street from Sun Sun's house. And you Know the old sayin'— once a robber, always a robber.'

My Partna, became suspicious of all the different cars, which kept pullin' up to Sun Sun's house.

Sometimes the visitors would be comin and goin, all thru the night, into the early mornin'.

And he knew from experience, that the only people that have that kind of traffic, are niggas that sell work.

So, he watched the Jamaican for about six months, and one night he notices a big U-Haul van, pull into the garage, driven by another dread-head.

He put two and two together and hit up Jay D and put him on the move. He said he wanted to hit the lick his-self, but it was too close to home— and a major rule of the game— never shit where you sleep.

So, here we are, in a low-key metallic-gray Ford Explorer, the new 2018 edition—Super Fast, Super clean—with the 180°-degree camera System.

You can't be drivin' no beat up hooptie, thru upscale communities, because you will look out of place. To keep the police off your trail, you need to drive somethin' new to blend in.

We drove pass the Jamaicans' house one time, and then parked at the end of the street, facin' out the neighborhood.

After 30 minutes of waitin', we look out the back window and see a G-wagon pull into Sun Sun's driveway.

Sun Sun, comes to porch and greet the man as he exits his truck, totin' a duffel bag.

As soon as they disappear into the house, we got out the Expedition, and make our way towards the home.

We all wearin' black clothes, to blend in with the night. We had planned on kickin' in the door, and hopefully surprisin' Sun Sun, before he could get to a gun. But once we saw the G-wagon pull up, it made more sense to lay on him to open the door, and then rush them comin out.

I was waitin' at the side of the house, closer to the door, and Jay D and Dae Dae, was duckin' down beside the G-wagon.

We rush the two men as they step out the door, onto the porch.

"Police! Don't move!" we scream in unison.

Startled by the three gunmen, they put their hands up.

"Hey! what's goin on?" Sun Sun said, shocked at seein' us.

There was no reply, as we forced them back into the house,

"Shut the Fuck up!" Jay D, states vehemently.

"Who else in here?" Dae Dae asked the Jamaican, while layin both men Face down on the carpet, wit' their hands laced behind their heads.

"Just my wife, upstairs!" Sun Sun, answers. "Please don't hurt her!" he begs. "I will give you everything I have."

At hearin' that, I run upstairs wit' my Glock 17, leadin' the way. As I get to the top of the steps, I see the bedroom door open.

"Atlanta Police!" I shout, as I enter the room, to keep her from shootin', as I come thru the door.

There was no one in it, but I notice the window open, and a pair of hands grippin' the window-seal, from the outside. I rush to it, just as the hands let go. I look out to see a woman get up off the ground, limpin' and runnin' away.

I pointed my Glock at her, but didn't shoot, in fear of alertin the neighborhood. So, I ran back downstairs, where I see Dae Dae, standin over the two men, pointin' his Draco at the back of their heads.

Jay D was puttin' stacks of money and pounds of weed in a curtain, he snatched off the window.

After leavin' them tied up, Face down, we grabbed everything we found and left.

Once we made it back to Summerhill, and started bussin everything down, we ended up splittin $750,000 and 200 pounds of mid-grade weed-plus the 30 pounds, the other nigga was buyin' from Sun Sun.

We gave the 30 pound's and $50,000 to our partna, for turnin' us on to the lick.

Before we separated, 1 told them what happened when I ran upstairs to get the wife, and how she jumped out the window— we had a good laugh at that!

CHAPTER 4

Danielle, and I, had a very good relationship, for the most part. We always were available for each other.

Date-night was a regular routine, somethin she implemented for us to stay focused on what really important.

If it was up to me, I would've suggested we stay in, and eat a homecooked meal, and afterwards, I would blow her back out, then we would've Netflix'd and chill.

This Wednesday, we are dressed to impress. she was lookin'' bad ass fuck in a body— huggin, white Dolce & Gabbana dress, wit Jimmy Choo stilettos. I was drippin' in a white Chanel shirt, Denim Jeans wit the Knee cut out. I had on the newest white Gucci loafer's wit the red and green stripes, to set off he red and green stripes on my white Gucci belt.

Both of us were drenched in VVS diamonds. All exclusively from Ice-box Jeweler, in Buckhead.

I wasn't trippin the dough, because I was straight from the lick had hit wit' my partnas, Dae

Dae and Jay D— which got my bag sittin nice, on almost a half a ticket!

A lil splurgin' is cool when you havin' your way wit the paper, so I bust down on a new Rollie.

The Sushi Restaurant, in mid-Town, is one of our favorite places to eat, we come here at least once a week, faithfully.

Sittin at our table, Danielle asks me how my day was, as we made small talk. I'm very tight-lipped about what I do in the streets: So, I told her I was posted at my store all day, and then I shot craps wit' the homies,

She knows I be hidin' shit from her, and she also know I do it for her own good.

It's not like I don't trust her, its more so out of habit, bein' from the hood, you learn what to say and what not to say. So, I learned early on that less is better.

Plus, the big-homies I came up around, use to always say to me: "keep yo' mouth closed, and yo' eyes open, cause loose lips sank ships." All I can say is, a lot of niggas didn't adhere to that rule, and so the prisons are full of niggas that talked too much. And whatever the jail didn't get, the graveyard did. Facts!

"Baby, you lookin like a young J. Lo," I told her.

"Baby please, I'm finer than J. Lo," she states, smilingly, "But thanks for the compliment."

I laugh at her sassiness. She then reaches across the table to hold my hand.

"Bae, you sexy tonight, too. Lookin like a young Idris Elba," she teases me right back.

I was still laughin' when the pretty Asian waitress came to take our order. Before walkin' away, she hit me wit a big smile and a lustful look in her eyes.

"Is there anything, I can do for you?" The waitress asks me, not payin attention to my girl, who was sittin across the table, mean-muggin.

I smile, "nah, that will be all. thank you."

"Yes, that will be all, Sweetie!" Danielle, sarcastically said to the waitress, who then hurriedly leaves to fill our order.

"That bitch is bold!" Danielle says while shakin her head, unbelievingly. "I thought she was getting ready to drop down and suck yo' dick right here at the table!"

I realized too late that laughin' at what she said, was the wrong thing to do but I couldn't help it, and only made her madder!

"And yo ass over there smilin' like the cat that ate the canary. You gone make me fuck you up." she say to me.

She then goes on a rant for about ten-minute about how aggressive and disrespectful these Atlanta ho's were. I knew she was really angry, because she flipped back and forth, between

English and Italian, I know it's crazy, but that shit sexy to me.

"And another thing!" she continues, "that Supa shit goin to get yo ass in trouble."

I look dumb founded at how the conversation had flipped on me, all of a sudden.

"Your arrogant butt lookin' crazy, like you don't know what's goin on."

I just shake my head and let her say her peace. Because I know if I say anything in my defense, it will only get her more heated.

Date-night started off smooth, but soon turned into a hell-date!

We ate our food, paid the bill, then drove home in silence.

While I was in the shower, Danielle got in and started bathin' me.

She grabs my face and kiss me before tellin me that we were havin a baby! She say she took a home-pregnancy test earlier that morning and was waitin to tell me over dinner— until the waitress pissed her off.

I was shocked and happy!

"I'm fixin' to be a dad!" I say wit' tears in my eyes.

"Yea, baby," she said and kiss me again. "And I'm goin to be a mommy!"

Now I understand why she went off at dinner, tonight. Her emotions are probably all over the place!

I picked her up and carried her to our bed. We made love late into the night, before driftin' off to sleep.

CHAPTER 5

Pullin' Out of Bailey's Rim shop, on Georgia Avenue. I'm in a 2018 Stingray Corvette, convertible, matte black, with red and black Forgiato's — Off-set 26's in the back, 24's upfront.

I decided to hit the road in it today, to show it off for the first time, after getting it painted, and mounted up.

I stop at a red light on the block, in front of M.L.K. middle school, and all the kids at the bus stop are pointin' their fingers and noddin' their head and approval.

I can't lie, it feels good to be flexin' thru my hood in this new shit! The older playa's like to see one of the neighborhood kids grow up and put on for the hood. So, I do it for them, as well as the young niggas, to motivate them to get money.

I see one of the big-Homies that took me under his wings and gave me the game, parked in front of the laundry-mat, leanin' up against the hood of his droptop Bentley.

Dino, is the son of one of the richest hustla's that came out of Summer Hill. His father was a heroin Lord, who also ran numbers, owned several nightclubs, and had illegal gamblin' and prostitution at his after-hour joints. But most of all he had a reputation for being a vicious, stone cold killa.

He controlled the hood from the 60s, up through the 80s, until he was sentenced to life in federal prison, where he ended up dying years later.

I park my car behind Dino's Bentley and get out.

"Aye, what's good, big-Homie?," I said to Dino.

"Nuthin lil bruh, just chilling," Dino says while clapping my hand and pulling me closer for a brotherly hug.

"I see ya Big dog! Let the hate begin!" he continues, referring to my Corvette.

Noddin my head, "hell yeah, I know they gone sehate. But fuck 'em!"

Dino, walks around my car, admirin' how I fixed it up.

"I like this bitch, I prolly need to knock me one."

"Yeah, it's hard, but I'm tryin' to power up so I can hop in shit like you got!"

A couple ho's walked by, and were sweatin' us, and our cars, tryin' to get us to notice them.

And once I was lookin', their walk became more sexier, ass jigglin' and bouncin' wit every step.

"Check this out lil bruh," Dino says seriously.

"I was kicking it out on the Eastside a few days ago, at my man Jig spot, on Gresham Road. He was saying some shit 'bout a nigga lil' Ced gettin' robbed. He said whoever Robbed lil' Ced, shot him in the leg with a stick, and they had to cut one of his legs off."

I listen closely, as Dino talked about the move, I brought lil' Ced in a few months ago.

But I don't show no signs that I know what he was talking about.

So, Dino, goes on to say that lil' Ced was saying how he remembered that one of the robbers had blonde dreads — and they both had red flags tied around their face.

I was shocked that lil' Ced saw my hair, because I had a black wave cap tied over my hair.

Then all of a sudden it hit me! When I jumped out the truck and chased him some of my dreads must've fallen out the wave cap, and I didn't notice it.

As my mind replayed the events of that day I was brought back to the present when I hear Dino say lil' Ced also remember the robbers driving away in a black Tahoe with tinted windows.

Dino, looks straight in my eyes, "now, I'm not saying it was you who done that, but it's too close to description to be coincidental, ya feel me?"

I nod my head to let him know I understood.

"I Need you to tighten up, and get rid of that truck," He advised me. "I'm not saying he gonna be on some hot shit and put 12 on you. But I hear the nigga got a lil money, so he probably try to send some hittas at you."

What Dino said made sense, and his warning had me thinking hard on my next move, as we parted ways.

I let him know I appreciate the heads up and assured him I will straighten it out.

It was a good thing that I ran into Dino today, or I would've been ridin' around in the blind — prolly wit' a ticket on my head too!

CHAPTER 6

It's been a couple of weeks since I spoke with my big Homie, Dino, and he put me on game about that nigga lil Ced.

I took his advice and got rid of the Tahoe. But you know how the streets are — everybody be talkin' 'bout who drives what? So, it probably won't be long for lil' Ced to find out who drove a black tented out Tahoe.

And once word got around that one of the robbers has blonde dreads — a hatin' ass nigga will be sure to scream my name.

But as usual, I'm one step ahead of the suckas. I have recently got a call from one of my homie's named Brizzle Hound, and he was lookin' for a plate, for him and his people to eat.

And so, I figured, before this lil Ced situation get out of hand, I might as well put him on the menu.

So, I told Brizzle once he got to the city to hit me up, so we could get together.

As I turn in the parking lot of Magic City strip

club, I noticed all the foreign cars.

Magic City Mondays are a ritual in the A— celebrities and dope boys, minglin' together, makin' it thunderstorm on bitches all night!

Walkin' them thru the door, I see so many stars, it looked like a B.E.T Award's show.

So much money on the floor, they have to rake it up at the end of the night.

Tonight, was Super Bowl Weekend in Atlanta, and everybody was here at Magic City, fuckin' up some commas.

I saw a Brink Truck parked out front, so I know it was millions in this bitch tonight.

Everywhere I looked, I saw money bein' thrown in the air.

Future's hit song, 'Poppin Tags' was pumpin from the speakers.

Every ho in here was Flawless- Magic City hires only the baddest dancers the city has to offer!

These ho's have mad followers on Instagram, and A lot of celebrities fly in to see them dance.

I bought an ounce of Moon Rock, from my partna, Bemo, and Fired up a blunt, so I'm vibin' right now.

To my right, I see Ralo and his fam-goon squad, makin' it rain on a bad ass red bitch!

She looks up to see me starin' and we lock eyes. I nod my head, to let her know to come holla at me, when she done dancin' for them niggas.

She was high yellow, bow-legged, six-pack stomach, like that bitch Ciara got, small perky breast, anda ass like Jacki-O.

This bitch was a stallion! No cap!

When she finished dancin for Ralo, she picked up her money and left the floor, Different ho's approached me askin do I want a dance, and after turnin' down a few of 'em, I finally said yes to a super-thick, chocolate bitch, that reminded me of Gabrielle Union- dimples and all.

I pulled out a thick wad of money, and put a twenty in her thong, before she stripped, and started twerkin her phat ass, makin it clap for me.

I was high as Fuck off the exotic I smoked, and the beat from the speakers had me caught in a wave, and I was throwin' money all over this bitch!

The more I threw, the harder she worked, but I aint trippin, because I bought a light twenty out, just to fuck up.

After about the third song, I felt someone tap my shoulder, from behind.

I look back, and it's the red-bone I saw I earlier.

I let chocolate know I was good, so she stopped dancin', and picked up her money and walked off.

The red bone, had changed into a black and gold Prada outfit. I could see her nipple piercing and clit-piercing, thru the material.

She leaned over and asked me my name?

"Supa, and for you to ask me that, means you new here, I state.

She looks at me in bewilderment.

"How you Know I'm new?" she asked. "And yes, recently just moved here from Philly."

She continues. "And who you supposed to be, that I should know you?"

Instead of answerin' her question, I hit her with one of my own.

"What's yo' name, shawdy?"

"Lucky" she answers with a smile. "And it's yo' lucky night that I showed up when I did"

"Why you say that?"

"Because you looked like you was goin' to throw all yo' money on that tree."

I burst out laughin' at her description of the darkskin, Gabrielle Union, look-a-like, that I let dance for me.

She pulled up a stool next to me and we chopped it up and got to know each other.

Before I left, we exchanged number's, with plans to hook up soon.

CHAPTER 7

Me and my homie playa opened up a weed-trap, sellin loud in Trestle-Tree Apartments, off Moreland Avenue.

Playa, had his baby mama get this spot for us in her name.

The apartment complex wasn't big, but this bitch was rockin—and this shit was full of ho's!

I was sittin in the livin room, playin the play-station, waitin for one of my traps to pull up, so I can serve him a few bags of O.G.-Kush.

I pause the game as my phone rings.

"Yeah," I say into it.

"Wassup Big homie?" Brizzle said.

Brizzle goes on to tell me him and his Blood Hounds were just gettin to the city, and they were ready to get it poppin.

They were some young hittas From Warner Robbin—a city an hour or so From Atlanta.

"Okay, say less, I say "y'all need to pull up."

I hang up and text the address to where I was.

Thirty minutes later, Brizzle was turnin' into

the parkin-lot. He was in a 2018 Impala, wit' three other Bloods.

Playa, stayed in the apartment runnin money thru the machine, while I met with Brizzle outside.

All Four occupants exited the Impala, and peac'd me up.

"Big Blood, what it do?" Brizzle says in greetin.

"Same ole shit" I reply. "Tryin to get a check"

"Hell, yeah bruh, I Feel ya on that: Brizzle responds. "That's why we up here. We tryin to see what's on the menu?"

During the talk I had a lil' while ago with my OG homie Dino, I learned that Lil' ced was really gettin paper.

Also, I Found out he had wife'd up a lil stripper bitch he met at a strip-club called Follies, on the north side of the city.

Had I Known all this at the time that I robbed him, I would've just kidnapped his punk-ass and made him take me to his stash!

After tellin Brizzle everything I knew about Lil' Ced, they said they was goin' to drive out to Follies and see can they find out some more info on Lil Ced's wifey.

They planned to lay on the bitch at work, and then follow her home, and wait for Lil' Ced to get there, so they could grab him.

"Or we could just grab his ho and make her call

Lil' ced, and have him pay for her back, Brizzle suggested. "But that would only work if here really cared for the bitch."

"I think y'all should stick to the first plan," I interjected. "It's more controlled that way, ya feel me?"

Everybody agreed, and the plan was set to rob lil' ced and then send him to his maker.

Brizzle and his homies said they would be gettin back at me once it was done.

After they left, I went back upstairs to help playa seran-wrap the money he counted— Plus, I had a couple move traps comin thru before we shut down.

I been at the Double-Tree Hotel, on Lavista Road, with Dominique, damn near all day.

We finally was able to be available to link up, after we had been talkin on the phone for a couple weeks.

She hit me up this mornin and said she didn't have to be at work until later, and so she wanted to spend some time with me.

We been fuckin for over two hours— ever since we got here, and she still ain't had enough of me.

"I want some more, she says sexily. "You said you was gone Fuck the air out of me"

She rubs her fingertips over my pipe, playin wit the pre-cum on the tip.

"Oh, you remember that day I told you that?"

"Mmhm," she nods her head, and then deep throat my dick. She gaged on it, and then pulls it back out, massagin her saliva all over it.

I then make her bend over, face down, ass up.

"Shit baby," she moans as I spread her cheeks apart and push my stiff pole into her swollen pussy. Her lips were slightly open from all the fuckin we had already done.

I start beatin the pussy and slappin her ass, makin it jiggle.

"Aaargh!" she screamed as I slid a fingerin her ass hole. "That shit feels good!"

Her ass hole clench on my finger and her pussy starts fartin out air, as she pushes back on my dick.

"I'm cummin on that dick"" she screams into the pillow, as I pound harder.

I grab her around her waist and pump five more times, before I pulled out and bust a load across her red ass-cheeks.

Leavin out the hotel room, walkin back to my car, I notice she was walkin funny, on her tip-toes— like her pussy was sore.

"What you lookin at?" she asks once she saw the smirk on my face.

"Nothin," I reply wit' a smile. "You aight?"

"Whatever," she says with a fake attitude. "You know you tried to kill my pussy!"

CHAPTER 8

Leavin' out of Fly Kicks, Shoe Boutique, on Peter Street, I received a call From Brizzle informin' me that he wanted to meet up with me. Asap!

I told him to pull up at the Red-Zone, and that I was on my way there now.

A Few minutes after I got to Summerhill, Brizzle pulled up. He got out the Impala, all smiles— with two duffel-bags in his hand.

I locked the store up and we went into the backroom, where I had a red-top, pool table.

"This your cut," Brizzle said, placin the duffels on the pool-table.

He then tells me everything went smooth and not to worry about anything comin back my way.

I didn't see any need to know any details. I was just happy everything went right, and they got away safely.

Nor the amount was any of my concern, because anything I got was love-but I could tell it was a good lick, because the bags looked full!

We chopped it up a lil' while longer, and then he left to pick up his homies from the hotel, so they could get back on the road to Warner Robbins.

I emptied out the bags and my eyes widened in shock and excitement at the contents.

One bag held six bricks of coke, four pounds of Moon-rock weed, and Five Pints of Lean.

The other bag held Five stacks of seran wrapped money.

The money had the amounts written ina black-marker on the seran-wrap— totalin' up to, one hundred thousand dollars— so that's 20 bands in each stack!

Damn! I just sat there shakin my head at the free bands I had come up on, wit' out even workin my gun.

My sister, Char, use to always tell me, "bruh, it's more than one way to skin a cat..."

Smilin to myself, I now see what she meant!

Later on that night, in bed with Danielle, we was watchin Fox 5 News.

The breakin News of the day was a couple found dead in their home, in College Park!

The reporter said it was a grisly scene, and that the motive appears to be robbery.

It wasn't a Forced entry, which leaves authorities to believe the murder victims may have known the intruders.

The reporter goes on to say both victims were

tortured before bein killed.

Danielle shook her head upon hearin' the gruesome details.

"Damn! Bae, I feel so sorry for them!"

I shake my head sympathetically at her statement, but I felt no remorse.

"See bae, that's why I be tellin you to watch your rear-view, and make sure you got your gun when you leave the house," I told her. "You never know who layin' on you to slip!"

She nods. "Okay baby, I understand"

Club Solutions was owned by one of the big homies from Summerhill, name Slim. He made it out the streets and now he's legit.

Slim, let the homies use the club to host events like, birthday- parties, Music-show cases, and any other functions we may need it For.

Tonight, we here to celebrate one of my partnas comin home from prison.

Felipe, is one of my day one niggas, and he just got released after servin six-years.

A lot of niggas are happy Felipe is back home, but there are some that Fear him, and wished he never got out.

Standin at 6'3, and 200 pounds even, he is a beast with the hands!

We were housed at the same prison before I got out, and we talked about all the noise we would make once we touched back down.

I had mad love for the homie, because I saw first-hand how hard he rode for Summerhill, and he was super loyal to anyone he called a friend.

He was the last of a dyin-breed! And that's why the whole hood showed up and showed out, for the gangsta.

We were in the VIP, surrounded by a flock of bad-bitches— smokin gas, and sippin Lean.

"Damn! It feels good to be home, bruh!" Felipe states excitedly.

I nod my head. "Yeah, I already know. I feel you big dog, I say understandingly. "That jail shit for the birds, not for playas like us"

"Straight up, son! He agrees as we dap up.

"Shout out to my nigga Felipe!" DJ Technic screams on the mic from the D.J Booth. "Welcome home, big homie!"

Upon hearin that, the club goes wild! Confetti begin fallin from the ceiling.

Lil Baby's hit song, Pure Cocaine, is pumpin thru the speakers. "When you rich like this you check the forecast, everyday it gone rain....

CHAPTER 9

Summer ended and Fall rolled around, coolin off the city. But, not without trouble-niggas had been murkin shit all summer.

I can't count how many funeral processions I passed by in traffic.

I was gettin a text-message every other week about somebody passin away.

Facebook and Instagram was on fire with RlP announcements.

Atlanta, was the new Gang-Land— this shit was goin hard like L.A.

Gang-Murders, everyday— then you add in drug-related homicides, robbery-related homicides, and just every day, regular non-sense-beef— this shit was the Valley of Death!

To make matters worse, you got these Good Fellas niggas runnin around the town murkin everything movin.

They're Known as The Mob. They have a strong hold on the west side of the city— from

M.L.K, Hightower Road, to Delmor Lane. They call that area, the Nine or 9th Ward.

The Bloods and Good Fellas are at war in the city, and it's a kill on sight order out on both sides.

At one time, the Bloods, and the Good Fellas co-existed, without beef-until they robbed an A.B.G member and murdered him.

"Blood, where you at?" I asked Smoke thru the phone as I'm drivin, to meet my trap.

"I'm on twenty, Bomin' back yo way" Smoke states. "I just left the Nine, tryin' to catch my man, ya feel me?"

"Okay, Bool. I'm in motion real quick, but I'll meet you in the hood when I'm done.

"Aight, say less," Smoke ended the call.

I'm on my way to the Bullpen, a Barbeque restaurant behind the Atlanta Braves Stadium.

I'm meetin' up with a nigga name Slick Rick, from Chattanooga, he lookin' to buy two bricks.

This my first time dealin' with ole boy-he use to cop work from my man T-rock.

T-rock switched his hustle from cocaine to heroin-so he plugged slick Rick in to me for the coke.

I'm a lil' early for the meet-up, so I can check out the scene.

For extra pre-caution, I had a couple hittas in a different car, already posted around the parking lot, just in case shit don't smell right-you can never be too careful in this game.

Twenty minutes later, I spot the gold 550 Benz as it turns in.

It parked next to my Matte Black Rover, sittin on Floaters.

Slick Rick, looks over at my truck, trying to see thru the tinted windows.

We both exit our rides, and shook hands, standing between our whips.

"What's good, playa?" Slick Rick greets me.

"Everything Gucci, my nigga," I responded. "How was your trip?"

"It was smooth comin' in, I just hope it be the same goin' back."

Nodding in response. "Yeah, I feel you on that!"

We continue to make small talk for a few minutes, to throw off anyone who may be watching us.

"Get in" I say, opening my truck door. He opens the passenger-door of his Benz, reaching in, and grab a brown paper bag from the dashboard.

He then walks around to the passenger-side of the Rover and got in.

"Here, big dog," he hands me the paper-bag. "It's all there."

I pulled out two stacks of money and counted

it quickly. It was 22 racks in both stacks— all hundreds.

"Everything straight," I say, confirmin' the money good.

I then reach behind the passenger-seat and grab a red MCM book-bag— containin' two bricks of coke-and pass if to him.

He said T-rock vouched for me, so he trusted my end was straight, too.

We shook hands and parted ways.

CHAPTER 10

We were havin' our once-a-week Blood meeting in the backroom of the store.

Lookin around the room, I saw angry faces on everyone in attendance.

And I also knew the reason why. Word got back to us about a song some Good Fellas niggas had made.

In the song they were braggin about how they robbed and murdered the homie, KayKay.

So, this meetin was about how we need to straighten them niggas for that death!

Bloody Tye, was sittin on the pool-table witha Draco across his lap.

"Blood, what's poppin?" Bloody Tye asked me.

"Murda on my mind, Blood you already know!" I say in answer.

"Straight like that! said a Blood name Five, who is also my cousin. "I'm wit' all the Fuck shit!"

"I'm ready to bang out on them Fuck niggas, Blood!" Smoke chimed in, pullin out his Glock.40.

I nod in agreement, lettin' everyone know that

the verdict is death for those responsible for killin' KayKay.

Bloody Tye, explain how we could catch them Mob niggas at a club on Simpson Road, called Deja Vu.

It's a favorite hang-out for the Mob on the west side.

Saturday came and we were two cars deep— four in each car— Me, Five, Chrome and Smoke was sittin in a black Malibu, while Bloody Tye and three other Bloods were in a black tinted out Durango— both whips were stolen cars.

We were in the Malibu, parked next to an excursion Truck, while the other homies were waitin' across the street in a plaza facin' the club.

A female Blood name Biara was inside Deja Vu, keepin' tabs on our targets— she would text me to let me know when they looked like they were leavin'.

Around 3:30 A.M. the text came.

"Come on Blood!" I say as Me, Smoke and Five, exited the car. Chrome, stayed behind the wheel.

The Excursion Truck hid us from anyone comin' out the door.

I had a FN, Smoke was strapped with his Glock.40, and Five wit' the 30 round extendo, Nine-Milli Ruger.

The club-door opened and out stepped three

men.

"That's Capo and Nooney" Smoke said, naming two of the three Mob niggas.

They stood in front of the door laughin' about somethin' and Fie'd up a blunt, oblivious to us behind the Truck.

As they start walkin thru the parkin-lot, towards a black G-Wagon, I step from around the Front of the Excursion, while smoke and Five cut them off From the back end.

"Wassup pussy!" I said and let the FN spit death. "Pop! Pop! Pop! Pop! Pop!"

I hit Capo in the chest with all five shots!

Smoke and Five, opened up on Nooney and the other nigga as they turn to run.

Two girls were just walkin' out the door once the shootin' started— they screamed and ran back into the club!

A few people that were in the parkin' lot, started runnin' for cover, while others ducked down where they stood.

As we turned to run back to the car, shots started comin' at us from a Cadillac STS, parked at the back of the club I ducked just in time, before a bullet smashed out the Excursion's side-window by my head.

I was able to make out the direction the gunfire was comin' from, by the spark of the gun as the shooter opened up at us.

The Cadillac sped out the parkin' lot as I returned fire— only to get cut off by Bloody Tye, hangin out the window of the Durango with the Draco spittin' rapidly.

"Boc! Boc! Boc! Boc!" Bullets spray the Cadillac, and it swerved and jumped the curb, crashin' into a parked car.

The doors swung open on the Durango as Bloody Tye, and two other homies get out and run up on the crashed Cadillac.

There was two men inside the car bleedin', but still conscious.

"This For the homie!" Bloody Tye states menacingly, before shootin' both men in the head multiple times.

"Let's go'" I shout from the window of the Malibu as we pull next to the Durango.

We sped up Simpson Road, before makin a quick left on West Lake Drive— on our way back to Summerhill— and away from the Chaos!

CHAPTER 11

The back and forth shootin' between my young niggas and the Good Fellas, had the streets on fire.

Things been mad crazy since we putdown that demonstration on them niggas at Deja Vu, a lil while ago.

For over a month straight, the murder of Five young men, outside a popular night-club, in west Atlanta was the top-story on all news-channels.

Durin' that time, I was stayin' out the way, and stackin' paper— lettin' the heat die down.

Bloody Tye, asked me to be in his new video for his song, Blood-In, Blood-out.

The crowd was thick on Haygood Avenue, in Summerhill, A.BG was on the set in Full Force-everybody drippin in mad ice and designer-gear!

I had on custom-made, American flag-chuck Taylors, with spikes on the toe and heel. Fitted Robin Jeans, with a red. BeBe belt with clear Rhinestones around it. A sleeveless Robin-Jacket, over a wife-beater with my A.BG-medallion hangin' from my neck. My Iced-out Rollie and 5star-earrings were dancing in the sun-light. I had my red bandana tied around my dreds.

For the video, Bloody Tye brought his new 2017 red Camaro, on 26-inch red and black Forgiatos. I had my stingray Corvette on display.

While we was finishin' up the video, the stripper I met a few months ago, from Magic City, pulled up in a Audi s5.

She got out the car lookin' sexy ass Fuck in a white Valentino body-dress, with gold Versace sandals.

I haven't seen her since the night I met her at Magic, but we did talk a Few times on the phone.

I walked towards her and gave her a hug.

"What's poppin' beautiful?"

"From what I see, you poppin!" Lucky, responds with a smile, showin off her beautiful Colgate-smile. "I didn't know you rap."

I shook my head. "Nah, I don't but my homie does," I say pointin" towards Bloody Tye.

"Oh, okay-I do remember seein' some of his videos on YouTube and World star. Ain't his name Bloody Tye?"

"Yeah" I nod.

Her eyes light up as she said," he needs to make me the main girl in one of his videos!"

I look side-ways at her.

"Damn, shawdy you ain't star-struck are you? Her Face screw-up at my question.

"Psst! Boy please. I ain't never that!" she denied. "I was just thinkin' of a check! strictly bizness, baby"

"Okay. I Feel you on that," I state, relieved that her not bein' a groupy.

In Atlanta you gotta be careful of bitches intentions, because there are so many celebrities and big dope boys around the city, and bitches be tryin to come-up off niggas— especially rich-niggas!

"Let's go get somethin' to eat," I say to her, grabbin' her hand.

But, before we left, I introduced her to Bloody Tye, and she gave him her business-card, wit' her name and contact info.

I had her follow me to my store, down the street, so she could park her car and hop in the 'Vette with me.

The Sun was out, so I dropped the top before we got on I-85, headed to Bahama Breeze, on Pleasant Hill Road.

We sat on the patio and enjoyed the Live-Band.

The evenin' was hot, but the over-head fans, hangin' from the rafters made it pleasant.

I was really enjoyin' her company, she was a good conversationist, and had me laughin' a lot.

I asked her why it took so long for us to hook-up? She explained how she was part of an elite group of dancers called, Atlanta Baddest Strippers. And, she said they be travelin' to different states, dancin, and a lot of time she not in the city.

Plus, there wasn't anyone special in her life right now-so it wasn't nothin' to keep her from workin' so much!

"There are so many beautiful women in Atlanta, so to be with a man here means you have to be ready to share him she further explains. "Women, out-number men twenty to one, and sharin' dick ain't my thing. so, I'm solo-dolo, right now.

I nod, in understanding.

"Yeah. I can dig it, lil buddy," I said. "I ain't sharin' my girl either."

She was starin' in my eyes while I was speakin' tryin' to gauge the truth in my words.

"And like you, I be grindin' so hard every day, that it be difficult for me to make time for anything else

Upon hearin' that she turns up her lips sardonically.

"You must think I'm crazy?" she asked.

"Nah. Why you say that?"

"Because there is no way your Fly ass ain't got no bitch you fuckin wit'!"

I looked into her eyes and said truthfully, "yeah, you right. I do have vibes I have fun wit'!" I explained. "But it's just that...Fun."

"I ain't mad at you, she responds. "I get it, you gotta release pressure sometimes, right?"

I nod my head, agreein'.

"Exactly"

The waitress, brings our meal, along with an apple-Martini for her, and a glass of sprite-soda or me

"So, what about you?" I inquired. "What nigga releasin' your pressure?"

She laughed at my question.

"Ain't no nigga releasin' anything over this way." She eats a bite of food. "And, if you must know. I have toys at home to play with"

"Mmhm" I groan, in disbelief.

"Mmhm, what silly?" she asked between sippin' from her glass. "You say that like you don't believe me?"

"Whatever," I say playfully "Only time will tell."

She nods in agreement. "Mmhm, For the both of us.

After we Finished our meal, we went back to Summerhill to pick up her car from my store, and then I followed her to her apartment in Riverdale.

I was in the livin' room, watchin' T.V. while

Lucky went to take a quick shower.

"You good?" she asked, walkin' back into the room.

"Yeah, I'm smooth"

She changed into a pair of black Lace-boy shorts with a matchin' Lace-bra. The sexy panties barely covered her butt-cheeks.

She had the type of ass that sat down her back, with that deep curve.

Every time she moved, it would shake and Jiggle!

"Shawdy, you sexy as hell!"

She smiles at my compliment as she sits down next to me.

"Thank you. Its hard work to look like this, she said. "But your fine ass already knows this"

Noddin' in agreement to her observation of me bein' physically fit.

"You look like you live in the gym, too, I say admirin' her six-pack abs.

"Yep. I got a membership at Planet-Fitness. But doin' all of them pole-tricks keeps a bitch tight, for real!"

She stretched out on the sofa with her head in my lap. I know she felt my dick gettin' hard under her head.

"You look like you give good massages, she said slyly.

"Mmmm...turn over, I said, orderin' her to lay

face down on her stomach.

"I hope you know what you doin?" she complied, getting' comfortable across my lap." Massagin' my booty makes me horny"

I start with her shoulders, before workin my hands down her back, until I get to her heart-shaped bubble-booty.

Her ass cheeks were so soft that my hands made deep imprints as I squeezed and rubbed each butt-cheek.

She moaned softly as my fingers got close to her lace covered lips.

She then spread her legs slightly, givin me a peek at her puffy print. I could see the moisture at the crotch of her panties.

Her back arched and her ass tooted up as I slid two fingers into the wetness of her pussy.

"Mumn...that Feels good!" she moaned as I rubbed the moisture around her clit.

She turned her head towards my dick, breathin heavy, makin my pole grow even stiffer.

"You feel how wet this pussy is?"

Her pussy was squishin, makin wet noises, soakin my Fingers with her juices.

"Stop playin' wit' it and Fuck me!" she begs me sexily.

She stood up in front of me and slid her boy shorts down her legs.

My eyes stared lustfully at the bald-headed

vee between her legs.

I quickly undressed and sat back on the sofa, hard dick standin' tall.

As I massaged my rod, pre-cum leaked out the head, and she bent down and licked it off.

I told her to turn around and touch her toes. I spread her bubble-butt and slid my tongue in the openin' of her pussy.

She reached around and grab my head, pushin' back on my tongue, makin' my tongue go deeper in her pussy.

"Suck this pussy, baby" she moans in pleasure as my lips are smackin' while eatin' her out.

I sucked on her clit and she start shakin.

"I'm gonna cum," she squeals, releasing' a wet- gush on my tongue.

While she was still feelin the nut she bust, I pulled her down on my pole.

"Ssss...shit! she groaned as she wiggled on my dick, adjustin' to my size, as she sat all the way down, until her ass was in my lap.

I reached around and pulled her bra up off her breast and squeezed her taut-nipples.

"You tight as fuck!" I said as she begin ridin' me.

"Mmmm... you got my pussy open!"

She grinds down hard on my dick, rollin her hips.

I lean back and enjoy the view of her fat, bubble-ass goin' up and down on my pole, spreadin' across my lap.

"Shit, I'm finna cum!" I said, grabbin' her hips, meetin' her mid-stroke, stroke for stroke.

"Aaargh!" she screams, "I'm cummin too!"

When I see her cum slidin' down my dick, I lose control and shoot my load deep inside her walls.

She collapsed on my dick that was still hard inside of her.

Smilin, she said, "I Feel you throbbin in my pussy!"

"Yo' shit Fie, shawdy!" I said, reachin around rubbin her breast, and kissin the side of her neck.

"Ssss... Oooh, that feels good baby. "She purrs as she rubs her finger across her clit. I want some more.

When she lifted up off my lap her pussy made a suction-noise as it released my dick.

Her cum was coated on my rod, and soakin my lap, where it leaked out of her pussy.

She laid on the sofa, legs open, revealin her pink, wet insides.

I placed one leg on my shoulder, as she grabbed my hard steel and placed it at the openin' of her slit.

"Aaaah!" she panted as I pressed deep into her softness.

I started fuckin her hard and fast, before I put her other leg on my shoulder, goin even deeper!

"Shit! Shit! shit!.. you so deep" She cried while bitin' her lip, from pleasure and pain.

As I feel my nut buildin, I pull out and have her bend over the arm of the sofa, so I can hit it from the back.

I spread open her ass-cheeks, so I can see my dick go in and out.

I slap my hand across one fat booty cheek, makin' it jiggle.

"Oh. My. God. You. Fuckin. The. Shit. Out. Me!" she moans after every pump.

I spit on a finger and slide it inside her asshole.

"Shit!" she gasped." I know you want this ass!"

Her freaky words had me wide-open, and I sped up, makin' our bodies clap every time I hit it!

She reached between her legs and massaged her clit.

"Nut in this pussy she begs me." I want to feel it!"

That's all it took to push me over the edge, and I squirt a glob of cum in her pussy.

CHAPTER 12

I was chillin' out in Summerhill when I got a face Time call from Danielle's mom, Ms. Maria, who everyone calls "Mo."

Her mom and sister had come down to Atlanta From New York, to be here For Danielle when she gave birth to our baby

Ms. Maria was a beautiful brunette, with a nice body!

Danielle's younger sister, Allison, was also a tall-stallion, and like Danielle, she had a big booty and hips.

Danielle's Mom and Dad, owns a truck-company in New York, and they contract-lease trash-containers to office-buildings, thru-out New York city.

Danielle was raised in a wealthy family, and her mom wanted to make sure I was able to provide a certain lifestyle for her.

Upon arrivin' at Atlanta HartsField-Jackson

Airport, me and Danielle picked up her mom and sister.

As we drove to our condo, her mom commented on how nice my Range-Rover was, and that she was thinkin' of buyin' one for herself.

It was their first-time visitin' Atlanta and she was takin in all the sights.

She was sayin' how everything looked new and clean-not all gloomy and old like New York.

Arrivin' at the condo, her mom walked from room to room, admirin' how we had decorated the place.

And from the smile on her Face, she was more than impressed!

They planned on gettin' a room at the Marriot hotel, for her and Allison, but we had plenty of room-so I insisted they stay with us.

So, for the last two weeks, they made themselves at home, and I knew Danielle was happy to have them there durin' her final stage of pregnancy.

"Hey mom, wassup?" usin' the endearment she insisted I use.

"Danny's water just broke and we in the truck on our way to the hospital!" she explained hysterically! hurry up and meet us there!" I could hear Allison tellin' Danielle to breathe.

"She can hear you, her mom turns the phone so Danielle could see me.

"I'm on my way, baby!" I said re-assurin' her.

She nods her head, bitin' her lips in pain, "Okay, she breathes out.

"I gotta hang up now, so I can get her there safely, okay her mom states.

I did the dash in my Hellcat challenger, runnin red-lights, and all.

I made it to Emory in record-time!

Emory Medical Center had the best pre-natal care in the country.

"I'm here baby!" I said enterin' her private room.

Her mom and sister were standin' next to her bed, as a Female-doctor sat on a stool between her up-raised legs, tellin' her to push!

Danielle, see me and tries to smile, but I could see the pain and Fear all over her beautiful Face.

A nurse brought me a Face mask and I held Danielle's hand durin' the delivery.

I whispered in her ear how much I loved her as she gave birth to our daughter.

We named her Khalina Nicole Flournoy!

She was a tiny replica of her mom, and I fell in love with her on first sight!

As she lay in my arms, I knew I had to go hard for her, makin' sure she had the world!

CHAPTER 13

Me, Smoke, Five, and Bloody Tye, was sittin' in Five's Pontiac Grand Prix. We was parked behind the CVS, on the corner of Ralph David Abernathy BLVD. and Ashby Street, in the west end district.

We are trying to catch a nigga name Big Twan that sold pounds of weed on the west side.

One of my partnas who new Big Twan, put me on the lick.

For the last couple of weeks, we did our homework on him, trying to see what his routine was.

My partnas Dre, told me that Big Twan had a convenient store in the west end, by the mall. We finally got a bead on him one day when he pulled up in a Bentley Bentayga. It was around 8:00 P.M. that he stopped by to lock up the store.

So, every night for the next two weeks we would drive over to where his store was and wait for him to come — And like clockwork, he will get there at 8:00 – and will always be alone.

The one worker he had inside the store will leave when big twin arrives, and shortly after, big Twan will lock up and leave also.

The plan was that tonight after he left at the store, we will grab him, before he got to his car.

Smoke, would hop in Big Twan's Bentley and drive off, while me and Bloody Tye would put Big Twan in the grand Prix, with us – where we would make him take us to his stash house.

"Blood, we gotta work fast!" stated Smoke, as we sat in the car waitin' on Big Twan to show up.

"Hell yeah, I already know. It's a lot of people still pulling up, too," I responded, lookin' at the different cars' driving through the CVS parking lot.

"And you know 12 be hot as fuck out here."

"Fuck 12! We gone blaze they ass if they get in the way of this paper!" Bloody Tye stated.

Glancin' around the CVS parking lot, I noticed two cameras on the side of the drugstore. Also, there was a couple more on the lofts to the right of us, that's on top of the shopping plaza.

"Y'all see these cameras?" I asked everyone in the car.

"Yeah. I already peeped that shit out, bruh," Smoke confirmed.

While I was sitting on the passenger- side, Smoke taps my shoulder from the backseat.

"Aye bruh, check out the Cadillac truck,"

smoke, said. Pointing towards the shopping plaza to our right. It was a 2017 Cadillac Escalade — black with 28-inch Forgiatos. It pulled into the parking lot of the plaza and backed in with the front facing us over in the CVS parking lot.

Thru the windshield of the Escalade, you can see the VVS diamonds around his neck and ears — and we were at least 30 feet or more away from him. At first, I thought he probably lived in one of the units in the loft, on top of the shopping-plaza — until I saw someone peep out the window blinds of a shoe boutique, where he just parked.

"Did y'all see that shit, bro?" I asked.

"Hell yeah! "Five stated, excitedly.

"It looks like somebody in the store was waiting on him."

"Exactly," I said, as the escalade's door open and out jump a heavy-set dude with dreads, totin' a duffel bag.

"Bruh, that's a play!" Smoke said when the shoe boutique's door open to let the man in.

"Either he serving them, or buying something from 'em," bloody Tye said.

"So, what y'all wanna do?" I asked them.

"We can wait on Big Twan, or we can grab buddy when he come out?"

"Shit bro, fuck waiting on Big Twan to pull up," smoke says.

"A lick is a lick. We got ole boy right here, right

now!"

"Hell yeah, Bruh, less rock!" Bloody Tye agrees. I nod my head.

"Alright then, say less, we are on it."

A few minutes later, someone peeped thru the window blinds of the shoe boutique, once again.

"He finna come out, come on let's go," Smoke says, exiting the car, followed by me.

I told bloody Tye and Five to stay in the car, since me and Smoke would just draw down on ole boy and take the duffel – easy and quick.

We made it halfway through the parking lot, when the boutique store opens, and the nigga walks out with the duffel bag.

He spots us walkin' at a fast place towards him, and suddenly we made eye contact.

It must've sent warning bells to his brain, because without hesitation, he pulled out a nine, with an extended – clip, and got to bustin' at us!

We had our guns tuck behind our leg, as we approach the Escalade, so as soon as the first shot came right our way, we up them and started bangin' back at the nigga.

"Boc! Boc! Boc!" I sent three quick shots at the nigga ass he dived behind the Escalade.

Smoke was hittin' at him as well with his Glock 40, before taking cover beside a park car.

All of the shooting has set off the alarms on the car as well as some of the businesses, in the shopping plaza

"Boc! Boc! Boc!.... Boc! Boc! Boc!" I squeeze off some shots from my Glock 17.

The nigga was using his Escalade as cover while he returned fire at me and smoke.

The nigga saw Bloody Tye tryin' to get out the Grand Prix.

"Boom! Boom!" the niggas sent two shots towards the car, makin' Bloody Tye and Five duck.

Seein' he was outgunned, he decided to make a run for it, and took off down the street running away from the plaza parking lot shooting as he ran! Me and Smoke ran back to the car!

"Damn! Let's go!" I say.

"12 gotta be on the way."

I could hear police sirens in the distance as we drove down Ralph David Abernathy Blvd.

CHAPTER 14

There are many reasons why the city is known as hotlanta – and one being the weather! Today, is a real scorcher, with a record high of 108°.

Me, Danielle, and our daughter, Khalina, are at White waters, on the west side of the city. The water park is owned by Six Flags over Georgia, amusement park.

The waterpark is so enormous, that it's nearly impossible to ride all the attractions in one day period all over the park, I see bad bitches! And they are wearing some of the smallest bikinis they could get in.

I'm trying not to let Danielle catch me looking at all the ass walking by us, as we lay on the lounge chairs, on the side of the resorts style pool. But I can't lie. My girl was killing it in a sexy, Versace bikini.

Her hair was in a tight ponytail and her lip gloss was poppin'!

Since having Khalina, her ass and hips got wider and the string bikini disappeared between her huge butt cheeks!

She had been obsessed with getting her figure back after giving birth to our daughter.

She hit the gym every day and dieting like a crazy person.

Her breast was now bustin' out the bikini top, and her round ass was sittin' up like two watermelons.

To look at her now, you couldn't tell she had given birth a year ago.

Danielle was laying on her stomach tanning, with her head restin' on her arms.

She was wearing a pair of gold Versace shades.

"If all these people weren't out here, I would dig that string out your ass and slide my dick in it!," I said to her, while layin' on my back with my daughter sleep on my chest.

Khalina, had on her a little Versace bathing suit as well, looking like a princess.

"I know you would, lil' nasty," she responded jokingly.

"You always trying to put something in me."

Two white dudes walked by and cut their eyes our way, sneakin' a look at Danielle 's bubble booty on display.

I had on a pair of Dolce and Gabanna shades, so they couldn't see my eyes, and they didn't notice I caught them admiring my girl's ass!

They continued walkin, as I bust out laughin.

"Damn, bae you got these white boys sneaking and geekin!"

"Tuh! Boy please, a white boy can't do nothing with all this ass!" she capped with a chuckle. "And you know I don't do white, so stop playing."

We both shared a laugh."

"That's right, all black everything, baby," I said, reaching over and smacking her ass, making it jiggle. "You my snow bunny. All this ass belongs to me."

"Mmhm... It sure does," she confirms sexily.

"My man black, baby black, and I got a black dog, too."

"And what else black? I asked her."

"That dick!" she said, sucking in her bottom lip. "Yo, you silly as hell!" I say, shaking my head at her.

"Yep. I know, but is still true, though," she replied. "Anyway, let's get back on the floats one more time before we leave."

CHAPTER 15

"Baby, you can be alone with your mom and dad, before I bring the baby over, okay"

I nod my head, sadly with a heavy heart.

"Okay, baby," I said, Kissin Danielle on the lips, as I exit the Range Rover at Lincoln Memorial Cemetery, on Simpson Road.

I'm Here with Danielle and our daughter, to visit my parents that they were buried here five years ago, side by side.

My dad passed away first from a heart attack, and then my mom, soon after.

The doctor said my mom died from a broken heart – that her will to live was weakened from losing my dad— her soulmate.

She couldn't live without him, and fell into a deep depression, that me or my sister, Char, couldn't bring her out of.

Aunt Melba said my mom wouldn't eat and begun losing weight. Aunt Melba said my mom just continued to lay in bed for days at a time.

When my aunt realized she was wasting away, she called the ambulance to come get my mom.

And admit her to the hospital. The doctors did all they could to help my mom recover, but after a month or so, she slipped into a coma – three months later she was gone.

Aunt Melba contacted the prison to get permission for me to attend the funeral, but they refused our request, again, the same as they did regardin' my dad's Funeral.

Since bein' home from prison, I make sure I come to see them at least once a month.

Tears flow from my eyes, as I prostrate between their graves.

"Oh Allah, please allow them entry into paradise, and allow them to be together, forever and always, as they were on earth, Aimeen."

I stood up after makin' supplication for my parents and motioned for Danielle and Khalina to come over.

I could tell Daniele had been cryin' in the truck, because her eyes were red and puffy.

"You okay, baby?" she asked, standin' next to me, holdin' our daughter

I nod, as I grab hold of Khalina.

"Mom, Dad...look who I brought to see y'all," I say. "It's Khalina. Say hi, grandma and Papa!"

Khalina, waves her little hands at the tombstones, smilin'.

Danielle was cleanin' off their graves and replacing' old Flowers with the new ones I brought.

When she was done, she stood next to me, and put her arms around me.

"Hey Mom and Dad! I'm still holdin on to the promise I made y'all the last time I was here," she said. "I will be here for him always and keep him safe."

As the tears Fell From Danielle's eyes she continued speakin'.

"Please keep watchin' over us and we will be just fine."

Later on...

After puttin Khalina to bed, Danelle and I were finishin up the dinner she cooked.

"Seriously bae, I ain't know white-girls could cook like that," I said jokingly. "You put yo' on foot it"

After placin' our dirty-dishes in the dishwasher, she walked around the Island-table and stood between my legs.

She lifted my chin to look into her eyes.

"Don't worry about what other white girls can or can't do, you understand me, Supa?" she said saucily.

I nod my understandin, runnin' my hands over her fat-booty, squeezin' each cheek.

"I see you need to be reminded that I'm a

special white-girl, she said as she dims the light in the kitchen.

She hops up on the island-table, and scoot to the edge.

Openin' her legs, she gives me a up close view of the pink Victoria Secrets G-string, that barely covered her fat pussy.

I grew hard and swollen against my boxer-briefs.

She slid the thin material to the side, and gently rubbed a finger between her moist lips, circlin' her clit.

"Ssss! Mmmm!.. look how wet I am," she moaned." I been fantasizin' about fuckin you all day!"

I pulled my dick out of my briefs, and it stood straight up, long, and stiff, as I sat in the chair. I was lickin my lips as she fingered her pussy.

"It's yours...taste your pussy baby!" she tells me, seein the lust in my eyes.

I grab her ankles and raise them to my shoulders, before droppin my head between her thighs, lickin up the wet trail that leaked from her pussy.

"Mmm....this pussy taste good!"

Danelle, grabs the back of my head and push my face and tongue deep into her pussy-a sign she's about to cum.

"Ahhh! Right there baby!" she cried in ecstasy, as I suck and flick my tongue across her hardened nub. "Aaargh! Aaargh! Aaargh!...Shit! I'm cummin!"

Cum, squirted from her pussy and splashed on my lips!

"Put it in me!" she told me, climbin off the table to impale herself on my steel-rod!

She felt like wet silk, slidin down my pole, her ass makin contact with my thighs.

"Ssss! Oooh!" she moaned. "Ahhh! you in my stomach!"

As she rides me, I'm grippin her ass-cheeks and kissin her breasts.

"You love this dick, don't ya?"

"Mmmm, Uh huh!" she panted between breaths.

"Make me cum, baby!" I tell her.

"Ahh...shit...You wanna cum in this pussy baby?" she started talkin dirty." Okay. I'm'a make that dick cum!"

She began grindin and rotatin her pussy around my length.

"You love this pussy...this fat, juicy pussy!"

She wraps her arms around my neck and start bouncin her ass up and down, twerkin' on my dick!

Her sex-tricks made me lose control.

"Shit!.. I'm cummin!" I groaned, releasin' a load of cum into her, fillin her with seed!

CHAPTER 16

Me and Bloody Tye was in the backroom of my store, shootin' pool, when we heard rapid, gunfire.

"Damn! That shit sound close as hell, bruh!" I said.

Bloody Tye nods his head. "Let's step outside and see what's up?"

Before leavin' out the door, I grabbed a Glock.40 from under the counter.

Lookin' down the street, I see all the homies standin' on the corner, lookin' up Haygood Avenue, towards Boynton Village Apartments.

"Aye K.T. what's goin on?" speakin' to one of the homies on the corner, as I walk up.

"I'on know, it sounds like it came from the 'partments," K.T. responded, shruggin' his shoulders.

"I'm finna drive up there and see what's up."

"Aight, let me know, I say."

K.T. gets into his black convertible SS Chevelle, on 24 inch-Bullets, and pull off.

A few minutes later, my phone rings.

"Yo, what's up?"

"Blood, you need to pull up!" K.T. spoke anxiously·

Me and Bloody Tye, pull in the apartments and get out.

There was a crowd of people standin in the street. Some were cryin, and others were shakin their heads in disbelief.

I crossed the streets to where K.T and a few other people stood.

"It's Lil Quan, bruh, K.T. said. "He dead!"

I caught a glimpse of the body and shook my head sadly.

There was so much blood around the body, as it lay half-way off the curbstone. And from how flesh and bone were hangin from Lil' Quan's body, I knew they shot him with an Assault-Rifle

"Whoever did it used a stick," I said voicin' my thoughts aloud.

K.T. nods at my statement.

"Damn! That's Fucked up, Blood!" K.T. Snapped angrily.

"Who would want shawty dead, tho?" I asked, perplexed. "He be all the way out the way."

"Chop, say he was comin' out the door when he saw a blue SRT Truck bend he corners and pull up on Lil Quan, while he stood on the corner," K.T. explained. "Chop, said he heard Lil Quan tell the person in the truck that he wasn't part of A.B.G. and he didn't know where they were, either."

Hearin this news, I realized the Killas were lookin' for us, so I waved over Bloody Tye, to hear what K.T. was tellin me.

After fillin him in, I told K.T. to finish explainin' what Chop told him.

"Chop, said the nigga in the truck said, "Well nigga you gone have to do," then he stucked the A.K. out the window, and gave Lil bruh, bout six of 'em, up close."

"It had to be them pussy ass GoodFellas, shawdy!" I stated, heated that an innocent man was dead because of some shit I might have done.

I knew they would try to hit us back, especially after what we did to Capo them at Deja Vu, about a year ago.

The big homies used to always tell us to stay on point, because in war, slippers count! And today the hood was slippin'— and we lost a real one.

Two weeks later, Lil' Quan was laid to rest at Southview Cemetery. It was drizzlin' which made the funeral even more sad, and dreary.

Standin' next to Danielle, holdin an umbrella over our heads, to keep the rain off. We were both wearin all black outfits.

I had on a black Chanel shirt and pants with black Balenciaga-shoes, and a red Ferragamo-belt.

Danielle was in a black Celine-body dress, black stiletto Red-Buttoms, and a red Celine-bag. We both had on dark shades.

Lookin out over everybody standin at the graveside, I could tell that a lot of people had mad love for Lil' Quan. And they showed up on this dark, gloomy day, to send him off properly.

"Baby, you okay. Danielle asked me puttin' her arms around my waist.

"Yeah," I nod and smile sadly.

When the Minister finished the graveside sermon and prayer, we walked back to the Rover and left.

Later that night, everybody met back up at Solutions, to celebrate Lil' Quan's life, and let some steam. The Big homie, Slim let Lil' Quan's family have the wake there.

It was packed, wall to wall! Everybody was Lit and turnt to the max!

Not only was Summerhill in the buildin', but people who knew Lil Quan, from other hoods, was also in attendance.

His Family got on stage and thanked everyone for their love and support!

Everybody in the crowd had on their 'Long Live Quan' shirts, in honor of a real Street-soldier.

The homie Chop, who witnessed the murder of Lil' Quan, was also a member of the Rap-group, Diablos — he hit the stage and did a rap freestyle in honor of

Lil' Quan, and when he Finished, you heard the crowd chantin', "Long Live Quan, over and over...

CHAPTER 17

My partna Fly, hit my line, and put me on a move. Fly, be trappin downtown on Broad Street, and he told me about a nigga name Monk, that be hustlin on the same block.

I remember Monk from when I use to come thru and Serve Fly. One day he told Fly he wanted to spend some money with me, so I made it happen— nothin big, only a few ounces of powder.

From what Fly explained, Monk's luck seems to have changed, as of two nights ago. Word was, Monk was out on Broad Street around 2.00 AM. trappin, when a S550 Benz Flew pass him bein chased by the police.

The lights on Broadstreet are mostly broken out so Twelve didn't see the black duffel-bag bein tossed out the window of the Benz.

Word was, Monk sent one of the Smokers who were out there to get the bag and bring it to him.

The next day after Monk found the duffel-bag, he walked up on my partna Fly, and tried to serve him some work.

Fly, said he thought Monk was cappin, until he told Fly to step into the variety-store on Broad Street.

Monk opened the bag and showed Fly what he had.

From what Fly saw, he said at least a couple bricks were in it, along with a few bagged-up ounces.

I was amazed that Monk was walkin around with all that dope on him— and that meant Monk didn't have a safe place to stash it.

Fly, said for the last couple of days Monk been flexin on niggas, actin like he the man on the block.

I ain't mad at him tho, because his flexin has put him on the menu to be ate. And I know I can't be the only nigga who heard about Monk's newfound wealth.

I told Fly to buy four and a half ounces from him, to make sure he still had it all on him.

"Yeah bruh?" I answer my phone.

"Everything's a go!" Fly confirms Monk still had all the work on him. "He left out, walkin' up Broad Street, towards Five-point."

Me and RaRa, was parked the next block over in the Grey Hound Bus, Parkin-lot, which was across the street from Magic City Strip Club.

We drove up Broad Street tryin to catch up to Monk, but the red-lights and the crazy traffic slowed us down.

Before we could reach him, he had made it to Five-points Train Station.

I thought he got away safe, until we turned down Forsyth Street, and I saw him walkin out the backside of the train-station— but he wasn't alone, he was strollin' with a thick red-bone.

I smiled at RaRa, "He must've come up here to meet that bitch?"

Monk and the woman had almost made it to the corner where they were goin to cross the street.

I observed all the traffic and didn't see a good place to jump out on Monk at, but there was no way I would let him get away, so I just prepared myself to do what I came to do.

"I don't give a fuck about none of these folks out here, or that bitch he wit'. I gotta have 'em!" I stressed to RaRa, voicin' my thoughts.

"Fuck it, Blood. Do you," RaRa said.

That was all the push I needed as we pulled up to the red-light, behind Monk, and his companion.

I jumped out wit my Glock.17 pointed at Monk's head. He threw his hands in the air as the red bone with him screamed and ran.

I wasn't trippin her runnin, I had who I came for.

"Here, you can have it!" Monk, fearfully gave me the book-bag, knowing what I was after.

"Nigga, get in the car before I kill you!"

I pushed him into the back seat of the Track-Hawk Jeep, and then got in beside him.

"You got it all!" he said as we drove off.

"Shut the fuck up!" I commanded, as I pat him down for a weapon.

"I promise, it's all in the bag. I ain't got no gun," he says.

Ridin thru downtown, we come up to a red light, and there were two motorcycle cops directing traffic.

"Nigga, don't even think about it!" I threatened him." I ain't goin to jail for robbery and kidnappin you. You might as well add murder to it, too!"

The light turned green, and we pull off without an incident.

I instructed RaRa to take us to Hill Street. Once we got here, I made Monk get out on the bridge.

After Monk got out, I made him run back the way we came. We then continued on our way to Summerhill, laughin' at how I just kidnapped a nigga in broad daylight, and robbed him.

I hit Fly up and told him to pull up, so I could break him off somethin' for givin me that sweet lick.

There was four and a half ounces already

bagged-up, so I gave them all to Fly.

"Good lookin, bruh!" Fly said, happy to be getting the free work.

After Fly pulled off, RaRa got his half of the lick— which was a brick and thirteen racks, and then left.

I put my brick in the safe I had in the backroom of my store and stuffed the thirteen-bands in my pocket.

I locked up the store, and pulled off in my Hellcat, on my way to Ice-Box Jeweler, in Buckhead, to drop the whole thirteen-racks on an engagement ring, for Danielle.

CHAPTER 18

Monday-night came, and Magic City Strip Club was turnt up'. All the different clicks were in the buildin', puttin' on for their hood.

Sparkled-up bottles of the most expensive liquor, and trays of money, were bein distributed thru-out the club, by beautiful women.

Usually, celebrities order their money from the club, while us dope boys bring our own money.

It's like Magic City, got a private stash of ho's that they swap out weekly, because as much as I be here, I swear I've seen at least five new ho's I ain't never Saw before.

To my left, was a crew of bad-bitches throwin' money, makin' it rain on a set of Twin-Strippers.

The Twin-Strippers, were Instagram-Famous, and they bring a lot of clientele into the club to throw big-money.

"Aye bruh, ain't that's your lil' vibe on stage?" Bloody Tye asked me, pointin' at Lucky and another

Stripper, doin' their routine.

"Yeah, that's her."

Lucky called me earlier and asked me to come thru. I told her I would stop by and fuck wit her for a minute.

I hit the homies up and asked if they wanted to mob out tonight? Everybody was on board, so we linked up at the Red-Zone, and then mobbed-out to the club.

We pulled up Five cars deep, four to each car. I was leadin' the motorcade in my Stingray, followed by Bloody Tye in his Camaro, K.T. in his SS Chevelle, Shell, in his 7 series BMW, and Five, bringin' up the rear in his Money- Green Charger, on 28-inch Ashanti's.

I was fresh as hell in Ash-blue Balmain jeans, with matchin Balmain jacket, and a wife-beater underneath. I had on Peanut butter Tims, with a beige Versace Belt, with the gold Medusa Head. Also, I Was rockin my A.B.G. medallion, and a plain gold Rollie.

The rest of the homies were Ice'd out and drippin in designer, too, givin these ho's somethin to see!

"Shout out to A.B.G!" D.J. Drama screams as soon as we entered the club.

I had 25-racks, stuffed in a beige Goyard-bag, I brought with me.

All the bros, had racks on them, ready to make a movie.

We got our own cameraman, who follow us around and shoot footage of us kickin' it. He then uploads the videos to our A.B.G. YouTube Page.

Playa rode in the 'Vette with me to the club. He is signed to our label, A.B.G. Ent. And when D.J Drama saw him with us, he started playin songs off Playa's album, 'Slime Season'.

And once some of the dancers realized we were in the club, they immediately came over to our section, and got to workin for the money.

We were tossin' money in the air watchin it fall on the strippers.

Playa was rappin' along with his song 'Money Gang', while the ho's twerked, and our cinematographer recorded us.

Lucky, finally made it off the stage and came over to where we were.

"Hey baby" she said exactly and hugged me.

"I see yall got it poppin over here!"

"You know how we do it!" I replied.

"Well, I hope you warmed up and ready for the main-event," she said with a smile.

"Today, my birthday, so I know yall gone show me some love."

"Ah shit! Happy Birthday, beautiful!" I exclaimed, giving her another hug.

She explained that's why the club was decorated in Lucky Charms-designs, which is her personal theme.

"Aight, say less, we finna make it Tsunami, just for you!"

"Okay. Let me go freshin' up and change into my birthday-outfit."

About fifteen minutes later, Lucky returned, lookin exotic, in a Lime-green thong with green three leaf clovers pasties coverin' her nipples,

"Happy Birthday, Lucky!" D.J. Drama shouted on the Mic, as she walked up the steps to the stage.

Jeezy and CTE, hit song came blarin' from the speakers. "Gone shake that ass bitch, I'ma throw his money!"...

Me and the bros stood at the edge of the stage and began throwin money in the air. So it fell on Lucky as she performed. Her pole-tricks were poppin and had the club piped-up. As she danced, her eyes locked on me and the message in them was clear.

I Followed her home after the club, and we made it as far as the Living-room, when L pushed her up against the wall, and fucked her standin up, with her legs around my waist.

We then showered, bathin' each other, before she dropped down, givin me head, as the water rained down over her.

Before I fell asleep, we had fucked at least three move times.

After I left Lucky's apartment, I stopped by my sister, Char's house to check on her and my nephew, Malik.

Charlita, who everyone calls Char, was ten years older than me, and since our parents passed away, she acts like she's my mom, instead of my sister.

Char is very over-protective of me, like our mother was.

I don't spend as much time with them as I like, and that's mainly because I be tryin to keep them separated from the things I do in the streets.

My nephew, Malik is Fifteen and a straight 'A' student, and because he's such a good Kia, I give him everything he wants.

My sister thinks I spoil him too much-always buyin him clothes and jewelry.

I'm just doin everything his dad would do for him if he were alive.

Malik's Father, Steve, was robbed and murdered when Malik was eight years old.

He was ambushed leavin a gamblin-spot on Boulevard, after winning a large amount of money from shootin' craps.

Steve was a big Heroin supplier from Fourth Ward, and he got rich on Boulevard, which was his stompin-ground.

That's why the rumors got started that the murderer was someone he knew, because he was robbed and killed in his own hood, where he was born and raised.

I had a lot of respect for Steve, because he took good care of char and Malik, and with the money he left them, Char was able to purchase her and Malik a Million-dollar home, in Buckhead—away from the slime of the hood.

"What brings you over here, this early in the mornin?" Char asked me as she got breakfast ready. "And why your clothes so wrinkled, your butt must ain't been home?"

Smilin at Char bein nosy questions, I answered. "Nah, I aint been home, and that's why I need you to tell Danielle I stayed here last night, after I left Magic City."

She put a plate of grits, eggs, and turkey-bacon, in front of me.

"Boy, I aint fixin to lie for you!" she exclaimed, shakin her head, disapprovingly.

I take a bite of the bacon. What you mean you aint gone lie for me?" I say. "You must wont her to leave me, then?"

"No, I don't want her to leave you. But you should've took your butt home last night!" she pointed out, reprimanding me.

"Just, if she calls you and ask if I stayed here, say yeah, okay?" I reiterated.

"Mm. Mm. Mm. Niggas aint you-know-what!" she exclaimed, before callin' Malik downstairs to eat breakfast.

"I aint a nigga, I'm your brother? I retort.

"And?.. You still a nigga with your dog butt!"

Maliks, walks into the kitchen.

"What's poppin Unc?" He greets me with a handshake and a hug.

"Shid, you already know!" I reply.

"Stop cussin' potty-mouth!" Char, admonished me, and me and Malik both burst out laughin, shakin our heads

"What you doin over here so early, unc? Malik asked the same question his mom did, which made me smile to myself.

"I can't come and check on m Fam?" I respond, "yall act like I need a reason to come by."

"Boy please...your uncle been out all night, bein his triflin-self!" she tells Malik. "And now he wants me to lie for his butt!"

"Charlita Nicole Flournoy...I begin, before she cut me off.

Uh uhh... don't call my name, baby. I know my name!" she exclaimed, rollin her eyes smartly.

"Khalif La'nard Flournoy!"

I just shook my head, knowin there was no winnin' with Char.

She's very stubborn, like our mother was, who was the master at arguing.

During the whole exchange, all Malik could do was look back and forth, from me to his mom, with a smile on his face.

He is used to us sparrin' over the years, and he knows the un-breakable love we have for each other.

After eatin' breakfast, Char walked me to my car.

"I got you, bruh, if she calls," she tells me giving in like she always do.

"I know, cause you love your chocolate-drop," I say smugly.

"Whatever...Malik my chocolate-drop, you a pain in the butt!" she said jokingly. "Be careful, okay. I Love you!"

"I Love you more!" I hug and kiss her cheek, before drivin home to face an angry Italian!

CHAPTER 19

Ever since the murder of Lil' Quan, the hood has been on high-alert, and we amped up security around the Red-Zone, because the "Ops" shouldn't have been able to come thru, hit nigga up, and then leave

I sent a carload of Bloods thru the 9th Ward to send a message. The streets were gossiping about the shootin, sayin a few people got hit, but no one died, tho.

We were all geeked up, ready to avenge Lil' Quan's death, and to 1 be honest, I was itchin' to bust my gun, just to relieve some of the pressure and stress I had been dealin wit' at home.

Danielle and I had been arguin a lot lately, and she even went thru my phone, tryin to see some shit!

I stayed out all night, a couple of months ago. and as soon as I walked thru the door, she went Kimbo Slice on me— hittin' me in my face and chest!

She was cryin, and threatenin to kill herself, and me as well, if I ever tried to leave her.

I just grabbed her arms and penned them to her sides, so she couldn't hurt me, or herself.

A lot of dudes think white girls are easy to handle, and not crazy like black girls. Whoever said that hasn't been with an Italian girl from New York.

But, in all honesty, I was to blame for her craziness. If I hadn't stayed at Lucky apartment after her birthday party at Magic City Me and Danielle probably wouldn't be beefin right now.

I had my sister tell Danielle I stayed at her house-which she did-but it was after Danielle had met me at the door, swingin on me!

She apologized after gettin off the phone with my sister, and gave me some of the best make-up head, I ever had!

But, I was still angry that she went thru my phone, invading my privacy and shit.

And to make matters worst, was the pictures and sexy videos she saw in it. She lost it when she saw all the black-girls I had in my phone, it struck a nerve!

"Oh, so you got a thing for black bitches now? she screamed at me. "So, what you doin wit a white girl, huh? your ass make me sick!"

I tried to make up some shit to tell her, but she wasn't hearin it.

So, it's been a war at home, and want to release my anger and Frustrations on somebody!

K.T. had his Lil brother steal a hot-box for us, and now we were in the dark-green Suburban, on our way to Delmar Lane on the Westside—the heart of 9th Ward.

It was understood that we was on a kill-mission, so we all had choppers.

"Let me out right here, Blood" I said to Five as we turned onto Delmar Lane, "I'm a creep up from the bottom, and catch anybody tryin to run this way."

"Bool," Five said, stoppin the truck so I could get out.

I was dressed in all black, with my red·flag tied around the lower half of my face.

The A-K47 had a pistol-grip, so I was able to hold it down beside my leg. It was pitch black dark, so you would have to really be lookin to notice it.

As the Suburban pulled off. I jogged up the street, in the shadow of darkness.

When I peeped around one of the buildings, I saw a group of dudes shootin craps, in of the breezeway.

I stood in silence, waitin for the shootin to start.

A moment later, the shots rang out! The machine-gun shots were loud and rapid, and the men stopped gamblin and made like they were headin' towards the shootin— not knowin that death was upon them, too!

"A.B.G. Muthafuka!" I shouted as I stepped from beside the buildin, shootin

Startled, the men looked back as the shots tore into their bodies.

One man reached for his gun at his waist, but was cut down by the chopper, before his hand could get it up.

I heard some doors slam closed, as people ran into their apartments, but no one come out the help the fallen men, as they died in the grass.

The Suburban was comin down the street, with the homies hangin out the windows, spittin death from the Assault-Riffles!

"Come on Blood!" Smoke yelled as the truck came to a stop where I was.

I got in, and we sped off, as someone ran into the street, bustin at us! The bullets were ricocheting off the truck, and knocked out the back-window, but none of us was hit.

"Fuck this!" K.T. said, as he stuck his Mac-90 out the window and started shootin back!

People were divin' to the around behind cars as K.T. sprayed at any and everything movin'.

CHAPTER 20

Today, is Danielle's birthday and I have a big surprise for her.

I knew I had to show her how much I appreciated all she'd done for me and our family

And I never forgot how she held me up when I was doin time in prison.

Plus, I had to make up for all the hurt I've caused her, so I knew I needed to go extra-hard!

Early this mornin', I took her for a birthday-Breakfast at Golden Corral.

She had no idea I had gotten a text from her mom and sister last night, to let me know they had landed, and were now checked-in at the Marriot-Hotel.

I contacted them a week ago, to let them know I wanted to fly them in to surprise Danielle, for her birthday!

But that wasn't the only present I had for her. I cashed out on a 2017 Mercedes-Benz C63 AMG, convertible, white with the black top.

Her mom and sister, plus my sister, were all in

on it with me. They were busy settin everything up, while I get Danielle out the condo.

We Finished up our food and was now back in the car, headed home.

"So, what you wanna do today? I asked innocently

"Ion kno, she said, shruggin her shoulders."

"It really don't matter, as long as we together"

"I was thinkin maybe dinner and a movie followed by some nasty, sweaty, hot birthday-sex!"

Shakin her head, and smilin, she said, "Baby, you get nasty, sweaty, hot sex, everyday!" I laughed, "Yeah, I do. But it don't be birthday-sex, and that's where the difference."

"Boy, shut up! you so silly!"

Char, texted me, sayin everything was ready. I responded back, lettin her know we were almost there.

Char, had picked up Danielle's Mom and Sister from the hotel, and we're waitin at the apartment for us.

"I'll get Khalina," I said un-fastenin her car-seat.

Since I was holdin our daughter I gave her the door key.

"Surprise!"

Everyone screamed in unison as we stepped thru the door! "Happy birthday!"

Danielle was so shocked clutched her chest with her mouth hangin wide open.

The tears begin fallin' from her eye when she realized her mom and sister were here.

They hugged her, and explained how I had set it all up for them to be here

"I Love you, baby! Thank you!" She tearful tells me.

"Oh yeah? Well you gone love me even more after you see your other present!" I boast.

"Follow me!"

Outside, was a Flat-bed truck, with the new Mercedes, I bought her on it. It had a red bow around it, with balloons tied to the side-mirror.

"Happy Birthday Baby!" I said, handin her the Keyless-remote.

She jumps up and dawn. "Oh my God!" she exclaims, over and over. "Thank you, baby"

"You welcome, bae" I was happy she loved her car.

Another reason I bought her the Benz, was so she wouldn't have to drive the Range Rover anymore.

Since I be driving it so much and bussin moves in it sometimes, it had gotten hot in the streets. I didn't want her and our daughter to be in it, and Someone mistakenly hurt them, thinking, it was me they were getting at.

Keeping my family safe is priority, everything

else is second to that.

We all ended up going to an early dinner at Gladys Knight Chicken and Waffles, on Peachtree.

Her mom said she had heard how good the food was in Atlanta and was excited we brought them here.

"I would've never thought to eat chicken with Waffles for dinner" Mama Mo said. "We Italians are big on Chicken and Pasta" she said between bites.

I thanked my sister Char, for helping me make this day special For Danielle.

"No problem. You know I Love Danielle, too, and would do anything for her" Char, replied.

CHAPTER 21

"This nigga is a real duck, bruh. I been on his humper For a minute," Smoke told me as we drove down Memorial Drive, headed to Kensington Station Apartments, in Decatur.

"You gone put your Face on it?" I asked, in a tone expressin my dis-like of the idea of lettin the nigga know it was him behind the robbery.

Smoke, nods his head. "Yeah, I'on care 'bout him Knowin t was me'? he continued. "I gotta let him see me in order for us to get in the door, ya feel me?"

Smoke, explained that he use to go to school with the nigga, and he wouldn't expect Smoke to rob him.

He said he had been buyin work from the nigga to finess him, to let his guard down.

Smoke picked me up from Summerhill, drivin his girl car, a dark green 2014 Impala.

I had my Glock.17 and Smoke had a Glock. 40, sittin in our lap as we turned into the apartment complex.

"That's the nigga Chris car right there, bruh, Smoke pointed towards a blue Maserati that was parked to the right of the buildin' that we stopped in front of.

"Aight bruh, you ready?" Smoke asked me while puttin his gun on his hip.

"Yeah. Let's rock!" I said tuckin' my gun.

Smoke gets out and walks into the hallway door.

Once he made it down the hallway to Chris door, I got out and looked down the hallway at Smoke, knockin on Chris door.

A couple seconds later, Smoke disappeared inside Chris apartment. I then opened the hallway door and made my way to Chris apartment door.

It was around 10 o'clock at night, so there wasn't anyone in the hallway to witness anything.

As I stood just outside the door, I heard voices on the other side of it, which let me know they hadn't moved further into the apartment, away from the door.

"Hey, is Chris in there?" a girl asked me as she came down the steps behind me.

"Yeah" I say, noddin my head, thinkin how I was goin to have to grab the girl and pull her into the apartment, once Smoke opened the door for me.

"Boc! Boc! Boc! Boc!" shots rang out so close to the door that I thought someone was shootin thru it.

The girl who was waitin at the door wit' me screamed in fear and took off runnin' down the hallway.

I quickly grabbed the doorknob thinkin it was Smoke doin the shootin, thinkin he had un-locked the door for me, but it was still locked.

"Boom! Boom! Boom! Boom!, Boom!" I jumped to the side of the door, realizing it was two different guns bein shot.

I tried For the doorknob once more before I backed up down the hallway, with my gun pointin towards Chris door, in case he came out shootin at whoever was turnin' his doorknob.

I made it out the hallway door and stood behind my car, waitin on someone to come out, hopin it would be Smoke.

I was surprised that no other people that lived in the buildin, had it come out to see who was doin all the shootin.

All of sudden I see Smoke open the hallway door and stumble out, He starts walkin' towards the car, movin real slow.

So, I rushed towards him, and that's when I realized he was shot and bleedin badly!

I helped him to the car, and that's when he tapped me and said weakly, "That's him."

I turned around just in time to see Chris comin out the hallway door, with a duffel bag hangin From his shoulder, and a gun in his hand.

"Booc! Boc! Boc! Boc!" I sent shots at him, and he stumbled, and shot back, runnin thru the grass and around he buildin.

I ran to the driver-side, got in and drove away.

Goin up Memorial Drive, the gleam from the Streetlights shined thru the windshield, and I was able to see how bad Smoke was shot up.

He was leanin over to his left-side, and his eyes were closed, he was barely breathin'.

"Bruh! You all right?" I panicked, thinkin he stopped breathin'.

"Nah'!" He replied, shakin his head with his eyes still shut, "Get me to Dekalb Medical," he whispered.

"Aight bruh, just hold on!" md as ran red-light, fearin we wouldn't get there in time, to save him.

As it was, we were at least 20 minutes away from Dekalb Medical—and speedin like I was, would surely get was pulled over, which would we bad for me, if he died, and couldn't clear me of his death.

I stopped at a red-light on Covington Hwy. and Memorial Drive, and he opened his eyes.

"Bruh, let me out at that gas-station," he told me, barely above a whisper.

"What?" I asked, confused. "Are you sure?"

"Yeah," he replied.

I turned into the Chevron, and helped him out the car, not comprehending why he wanted to get out there.

"Now go, bruh!" he instructed me.

I didn't think twice why he was tellin me to leave him. I pulled off, hoping he was makin the right decision.

I looked over at the passenger-seat and saw it was soaked with Smoke's bloods, as well as the car-mat and cup-holder, too.

I shook my head, thinkin of all the blood he lost and that he might not survive.

Finally, I made it to my sister house, without bein pulled over, I called and told her I was on my way there, so she was on the porch when I pulled up.

"Oh my God! Why are you covered in Blood?" she asked hysterically when I got out the car. "Are you hurt?"

I shook my head.

"This Smoke's blood," I tell her as we enter, her house, "He was shot!"

"Wh...why? What happened?" she stammered.

I patiently explained to Char, every detail of what took place, startin from the beginning, leadin up to smoke tellin me to let him out at the Chevron gas-station.

Char, sat next to me, clearly in shock from all that I told her.

"Do you have cleanin-supplies?" I asked her, breakin the silence, "I need to clean the blood out the car."

"Yeah. Hold up," she answered.

She returned with a bucket of water, washin-powder, and bleach.

As we cleaned the car, she asked me did I think Smoke will be, okay?

I shook my head sadly.

"I don't know, Sis. He was hit bad!" I said voicin my worst fears.

"Well, we gone pray for him. God is in charge!" she said to me, as she smiled, tryin to re-assure me everything would be fine.

We got most of the blood up, but the smell of blood was still strong in the air.

My sister went into the house to throw away the Blood-towels and put away the cleanin-supplies.

"I don't think you should drive home with them guns in the car with you, she tells me as I got ready to leave. "Leave 'em here. I'll put 'em up. Just come get 'em later, okay."

What she said made sense, so I went to the car and reached under the front-seat and grabbed my Glock 17. And then it came to me in a Flash; what did Smoke do with his gun? I don't remember seein it when I helped him to the car, or when he got out at the gas-station.

I started searchin up under the passenger-seat, thinkin he might have dropped it when he sat down, but no, it wasn't there.

All of a sudden, I remembered two different guns firing inside of Chris' apartment.

Damn! Could Chris have somehow gotten Smoke's gun, and shot him with it? I thought to myself.

Or did Smoke still have it on him when he got out the car? I was still tryin to come up with an answer to those questions as I drove home, leavin the Glock 17 with my sister.

CHAPTER 22

Last night after I got home, Daniele was panickin and upset when she saw me covered in blood.

I couldn't lie to her, so I ended up telling her what happened. We called around to all the hospitals in the city, trying to locate Smoke.

I felt guilty for leaving him like he asked me to, but for real, I knew I couldn't risk staying and being arrested, if he didn't survive— or that nigga Chris, who I assumed I shot, died.

Even though I was mentally drained and physically tired, I couldn't sleep until I knew something about my homie.

I watched the news on different stations all night. finally, around six in the morning there was a report about a shooting victim that walked into a Chevron gas-station and collapsed.

It was said that luckily for him there was a DeKalb County Sherriff sitting in his patrol car outside the Chevron. The Sherriff was able to revive and sustain the life of the gunshot victim, until paramedics showed up and transported him to a local hospital.

The reporter also said that the authorities said they wanted to thank the good Samaritan who dropped the victim off at the gas station, because in doing so, saved the victim life.

I drifted off to sleep after hearing Smoke was alive.

Later that day, I was out in Summerhill letting the homies know what happened to Smoke, and that he was okay so far.

Before I left home that morning, I had called Smoke's sister, Biara, and she was able to get more info on her brother's condition.

She said Smoke was Flown to Grady Memorial Hospital, where they have one of the best Trauma Centers in the city.

"So, he should pull through this shit, right?" Bloody Tye asked me.

I nod my head in answer, still un-believing what happened last night.

"Damn! I don't understand what went wrong," I say remorsefully.

Five, shook his hand. "Yeah, that shit Brazy!"

"I don't give a fuck what happened.

I wanna go back out there and rock that boy. You say you hit the nigga, right?" K.T. stated vehemently.

"Yeah, he stumbled when I squeezed on 'em comin' out the door, I explain.

"Then he shot back and hit the corner of the building runnin."

Shell's BMW pulls up next to my Range Rover and him and RaRa gets out, peace'n everybody up.

"What's pop'n Blood?" RaRa asked me. "How Smoke doin?"

"He's doin' good so far, his sister said he was in surgery all mornin'."

"Bool" RaRa nods at the good news,

"How Biara doin? I know she wiggin' bout her bro!"

I shake my head, sadly, "Yeah, but you know she a soldier she gone stay strong for the bro."

Shell and RaRa, was gone slide over to Kensington Station Apartments, and see if they can find out if Chris was shot, and if so, did he survive or not?

"I gotta lil vibe out there I be fuckin with I'ma pull up on her and see what she can tell me" Shell explains.

"That bitch keep her ear to the streets."

"Aight, say less," I respond, as they pull off in the 7 series.

"When we gone be able to see Smoke?" Five asked.

"I'on know bruh, hopefully soon. Biara, said she gone let me know, I answer.

CHAPTER 23

"I'm gone stop over your way when I leave my friend house, so don't go nowhere," Dominique tells me.

"Aight bae, I'll be here, I say hanging up the phone. I was in the back of my store shooting pool with my nephew Malik.

I was letting him hang out with me today, after I picked him up from school and took him shopping at Greenbriar Mall, over in the SWATS.

He had been asking for the Gold and Black Lebron James. I promised him if he got mostly A's on his report-card, that I would buy them for him.

Malik, is so smart he ended up getting al A's them Lebrons, I got him two more pairs of shoes— some Red and Black Penny Hardaway's, and some Lime-green Kobe's.

"I hope that wasn't my mom you was talkin' to," Malik jokingly, before taking a shot at a ball.

I laugh, knowing he was thinking his mom might be on the way to get him. He loves his mom, but says she's a vibe killer, and don't like for him to be over in the hood.

"Nah, that's my lil vibe, Dominique. She finna stop by for a second," I assure him.

"Damn Unc, you got all the action!" I bust out laughing at Malik's words, "Shid, I ain't the only one, from what ya' mom tells me. She said your Instagram be pop'n, and you be up all night talkin' to girls."

Hearing me say that, makes Malik grin.

He then rubs on his beginner's goatee. "Aye, I got it honestly, ya feel me?" He arrogantly state." I can't help they like my drip."

I smile, thinking how proud his dad, Steve, would be to see how Malik turned out. "Yeah, I hear you Fly guy" I teased him." Just make sure you protect your drip or your mom gone kill me and you, both!"

Char, swears I'm the reason Malik acts the way he does. She says he's trying to be like me, His username on Instagram is young Supa.

I got a text from Dominique saying she just pulled.

"Go let her in, Malik."

A few minutes later, Dominique walks in, followed by Malik.

I introduce them to each other after giving Dominique a hug.

"Hi Malik!" she says. "He's cute!"

I smile as Malik blush at her compliment. He was giving her his best Mack daddy pose.

"I know you got all the lil girls at the school goin' crazy." She continues to inflate his ego.

"I do a lil some some, ya feel me?" Malik pop back like a true player.

I leaned against the pool table and watched how my nephew handled himself with a bad bitch like Dominique.

For everything Dominique said to him, he had a slick response. I admired how he didn't freeze up, tongue-tied, when a bitch got on his bumper.

I shook my head, thinking how Char, had no idea that Malik was very mature for his age.

Malik had Dominique blushing like a schoolgirl, showing her dimples.

"Mm. Mm... he gone be hell when he gets older!" Dominique acknowledges Malik's game.

I nod in agreement.

"Aye Malik, go hold the register down for me," I instruct him.

"Aight Unc." He leaves us alone, shutting the door.

"So, what brings you to my neck of the woods?" I asked her.

"Your neck of the woods? You must have forgot, this is my neighborhood, too!" she retorts. "I'm Summerhill, for real"

Laughing at her response, I pull her between my legs as I kiss her lips.

"Nah, I ain't forgot."

"Well, first off, I miss you, and secondly, I heard Smoke got shot!"

"I miss you too! It's been a minute since I saw you." I say. "And hopefully, Smoke be alright."

She nods her head sadly and squeeze me tightly.

"I know how close y'all are, thank God you wasn't hurt?"

"Yeah, that's my lil bro for real!"

I changed subjects to keep from getting super emotional about it. Also, I knew in my heart Smoke would be fine. But by chance he wasn't, I was prepared to turn Kensington Station Apartments into a graveyard.

"What you been up to lately? I asked her.

"Nothin', just working hard every day."

"And what do you have on?" I say admiring her outfit getting a good view of her body hugging top and skintight jeans.

"Damn! You Fine ass fuck!" I state, lustfully, as I pulled her back to me, why haven't you gotten back with me since we last hooked up?" she asked with an attitude.

"I'm sorry for that, too!" I explain.

"It's been so much goin on, that I got caught up"

"Well, you know I be tryin' to fuck with you on some real shit" she lets me know. "And I don't want it to just be on some sex shit either.

I stared into her eyes, trying to gauge the truth of her words.

It's hard coming from the streets to trust women, but I know Dominique to be a good girl, wifey material. She didn't have a bad name in the streets and couldn't think of any other nigga around the hood that had smashed her besides me.

"I want fuck with you too," I admit. "Matter fact, we should go on a date this weekend, if you free?"

She smiles and nods her head, "I would like that very much I'll text you my address."

"Aight, I'm lookin' forward to it."

We kicked it a while longer before I walked her out front to leave.

"Bye, Malik!" she waves to my nephew while exiting the store.

"Later," Malik, responds all cool and shit.

CHAPTER 24

I picked Dominique up from her condo, and we had a nice dinner-date at Fellini's on Ponce De Leon.

We were now driving up Moreland Avenue, on our way to starlight Drive-In Movie, to see the new movie, Queen and Slim.

"I been waitin to see this movie, but I didn't have anyone to go with!" Dominique told me excitedly.

"I saw the pre-view for it, so it should be fine." I reply.

Dominique was looking sexy and stylish in skintight jeans, with a short black leather jacket. She was also wearing black Valentino pumps.

I was fresh in Fendi, from head to toe.

I parked on a spot away from the other movie watchers, so we could have some privacy, she took off her heels and slid her back to get more comfortable, and I did the same.

"Don't have my truck smellin' like Cheetos!" I teased her.

"Boy please! My feet don't stink!" she laughed and hit me playfully on the shoulder.

"Whateva, I'll be the judge of that"

She then turns sideways and place her feet on my lap. Her toes were French manicured and sexy. I was massaging her feet as the movie started to play. Actually, I noticed her feet smelled like Mango.

"Mmm... that feels good!" she moans

"Oh, you like that?" she nods her head, closing her eyes in rapture.

"You better open your eyes before you miss the movie, I warn her.

"I can't concentrate while you rubbin my hot spot"

"Oh yeah? Well, how this feel? I kissed and licked each toe.

Her eyes rolling in ecstasy, was the answer to my question.

"Baby, you better stop before we both miss the movie!" she says lustfully. "My pussy is so wet, right now!"

At hearing her confession, my dick instantly gets hard. "Fuck the movie, I wanna taste this pussy!"

We both climbed in the backseat and she undressed as I took off my pants and shoes, I got between her thighs and placed one of her legs on my shoulder.

"Shit. You so big!" she said, grabbing hardness, rubbing the head between her pussy lips, wetting my tip with her juices.

The tint on my truck prohibits anyone from seein us.

I bite down on her hardened nipple, as I push deep into her tight wetness.

"Aaargh! she screamed, as her pussy opened for me. "Ssssh...you at the bottom!" I grind deep, rolling my pelvis, hittin her corners.

She grabs my head and bring my lips to hers for a deep kiss.

"This dick good, aint' it?"

"Uh huh...ssss!" she bites her bottom lip in pleasure.

"I want to taste it!" I pull out and slide lower to lick on her wetness.

She lifts one leg over my shoulder while I'm licking and tongue-fucking her pussy.

"Ahhh!... I'm gonna cum!" she exclaims.

I place two fingers in her pussy and rotate them, while I'm sucking on her swollen nub.

"Here it comes... here it comes!" she chants. "Aaargh!" she gushes all over my lips and fingers, and I lick it up.

I had her turnover and lay on her stomach, with one leg leaning on the floor of the truck.

I spread her ass cheeks and slid my throbbing dick into her drenched pussy. I begin pounding hard, making our bodies smack loudly, as I contacted her bubble booty.

"Ah. Ah. Ah!" she moaned. "This your pussy!"

I was so turned on from her moans. I put one hand around her neck, and gripped the backseat for balance, with the other one.

"Yes baby!... Fuck your pussy!" she commanded me. "Make it talk baby!"

I felt my nut building up, as she talked nasty.

"Shit!.. Ahhh..!" I groaned, busting my nut deep inside her soppin wet pussy.

Dominique, starts rolling her ass and grinding back on me, as she felt my cum coating the insides of her walls.

"Mmmm... Yes. I want it all!" she used her pussy muscles to squeeze out every drop of cum.

She had a big smile of satisfaction on her lips, as I pulled my semi-hard dick from her pussy.

I laid my dick between her butt cheeks, and squeezed out a thin trail of cum, and rubbed down her crack.

"Boy, you so nasty," she said with a laugh.

"Mmhm... I sure am." I agree.

"Don't move," I say as I reach into my glove-compartment for some wet wipes.

"Use these," I say handing her some wipes.

She wiped up the trail of cum from between her hefty cheeks, and also between her pussy lips.

"I hate to ask...but why do you have wet wipes in your dashboard?"

I laughed at her question, because I knew she was probably thinking the wipes were for the purpose of cleaning up after Fuckin bitches in my truck— which was far from the truth.

"Definitely not for what you thinkin." I explain." Sometimes I be eating and drinking in here, and in case I spill something, I can clean it quick before it stains my seats."

Nodding her head at my explanation.

"Oh, o.k. I was finna say, don't make me eff you up," she sounded relieved at my answer.

We were able to watch the last 30 minutes of Queen and Slim, and then we left.

"I'm gone text you when I wake up," she said before exiting my truck at her apartment. "Be safe, okay?"

Aight bae, I had fun tonight," I reply.

"Me too!" Dominique smiled blowing me a kiss, before walking into her door.

CHAPTER 25

"Me and my mom just left the hospital. Everything is still the same."

Biara was telling me on the phone Smoke, was still ina coma. He had been medically induced. For over 2 months. The doctors said they had to do that in order for his body to heal and repair itself, without all the pain from the gun shots.

Ever since Smoke been in the hospital, me and a few homies have been sliding out to Kensington Station Apartments trying to catch Chris, as of yet, we haven't had any luck.

Shell, said his stripper friend told him that she heard Chris was shot in the shoulder that night and that he was already out the hospital.

Evidently he was in hiding and haven't been back to his apartment since the robbery attempt.

Also, I knew the streets done told him that some niggaz was looking for him,

"I appreciate y'all lettin' me know how Smoke doin', I tell Biara.

"All the time big homie" she replied.

"I know you waitin' to go see him!"

"For real, I responded, "This shit ain't been the

same without him!"

Before hanging up. I told her to let her Mom know to call me if she needs anything.

When Danielle heard me say goodbye to Biara, she entered our bedroom with our daughter in her arms.

"Baby, you ok?" she sits down next to me on the bed and gives me a kiss.

"Yeah, I'm good. Just finished talkin to Biara checkin' on Smoke."

"How he's doin?"

I shake my head sadly.

Still the same, I answer.

"Well, we gone keep prayin', Ain't that right Lina," she states, while

Kissing Khalina on her cheeks making her laugh,

"Oh, I almost forgot to tell you that I found a good daycare for her."

Danielle continues. "It's about 25 minutes from here, in Sandy Springs."

"Okay, that's Bool, just make sure they have A-1 ratings, ya feel me?"

Rolling her eyes at me, she states.

"I know ain't nothing but the best for our cream puff Princess," she said.

Laughing at her fake attitude at how over-protective I am over our daughter.

"Somebody sounds jealous of daddy's pretty

baby,' I say jokingly, as I grab Khalina out of Danielle's arms.

"Boy, whateva! Never that," she exclaimed. "You know a happy wife means a happy life!"

She gets up to gather up the dirty clothes throw them in the washer.

I get up with our daughter so she can grab the comfort off the bed, and as she bends over I slap her booty to make it jiggle.

"Look at you... nasty man!" she giggled and did a lil twerk, making her ass jump.

Seeing all that ass bounce had me getting instantly hard. She saw my bulge in my brief.

"Come on Lina, let's play with your doll-house," she walked our daughter to her bedroom leaving Khalina in her room playing with her dolls, Danielle rushes back into our room.

Grabbing my hand, she pulls me into our bathroom,

"Harry up, before she come lookin' for me!"

She bends over on the sink counter, reaches back, and pulls her thong aside, showing me her fat shaved pussy.

I squat down and lick between her moist lips, sliding my tongue into her pussy.

My dick didn't need any stroking, it was standing tall and strong. I eased the head in first, and then pushed all the way, until her ass cheeks was pressed against my pelvis

"Ssss...Shit!" she moans in ecstasy. "Fuck your pussy daddy!"

I grab onto her hips and stroke long and hard.

In seconds, her pussy became super wet, making a squishing noise.

"Uhhh! Fuck! I'm finna cum!" she screams, and cream all over my pole

I pulled my cum covered dick from her pulsating pussy, and rub it between her ass crack, lubricating her ass hole with her cum.

I use my thumb to push some wetness into her hole, making her squeal out in pleasure. "Aaahh!"

"Mmhm... You like that shit don't you?"

I say, slidng my dick back into her pussy.

"Ssss...Mmm...you know I do!" she admits. "I want you to fuck my ass!"

The nastier she talked, the harder my dick got.

"Wet that dick and fuck my ass daddy!" she begged me lustfully.

My dick was drenched as I pulled it from her pussy. I put the tip in her asshole and pushed it in, feeling the tightness grip my dick.

"Shit! she screamed as I opened her asshole to accommodate my thickness.

"Oooh...Fuck!"

I started off pumping slow, and she was rubbing her clit, making her ass and pussy wet at the same time.

She began throwing it back as I fucked her ass.

"Mmm...cum in this ass baby!" she instructed me.

Looking at my pole as it drove deep into her ass, had me geeked up, and I sped up, hitting it hard.

"Here it comes baby!" I tell her squirting cum deep inside her ass hole.

When my dick stops pulsating I pull out, still hard.

"Damn! You an animal bae!" Acknowledged her fire sex game, shaking my head.

"You ain't gotta tell me baby. I already know that," she said with pride. "Now, go check on your daughter, while I get in the shower."

Walking back through my bedroom to check on my daughter, my phone starts ringing, and I reach to grab it off the bed I see my big homie's name on my screen.

I was dreading this particular call from him, because of the situation with the homie Smoke.

I knew that one way or another the news of al the shit the hood would reach his ears. Usually, I hit his line to update him on what's pop'n with the homies, so for him to be hitting my line, tells me this call ain't good.

"Wooh! What's Rollackin' big homie?"

"Wooh!" Was the response from the big homie Nasty. "Us Fuck them!"

ABOUT THE AUTHOR

Born and raised in Atlanta Georgia, the Summerhill neighborhood of zone three. OLA Ken, transition from the trenches to become a legitimate business owner. He's also a motivational-speaker and is in the process of starting a nonprofit organization. Adding to his already extensive, personal achievements, OLA Ken it is now a self-published author.

Made in the USA
Middletown, DE
05 January 2023